Dear Reader

Revenge can be a powerful motivator—we witnessed that in *Stolen by the Sheikh,* where Sheikh Khaled settled an old score with his foe, Paolo Mancini. Khaled stole Paolo's girlfriend, Sapphire Clemenger, for his wife.

In the same way, loss can drive people to extreme actions. Paolo has now lost too much to lose any more. In quick succession both his father and now his girlfriend have been stolen from him. There's no way he's going to risk losing anything or anyone more.

The Mancini Marriage Bargain is Paolo's story, and tells of his reunion with Helene Grainger, the woman he saved from the Sheikh's grasp so long ago. The consequences of their passionate reunion provide another reason he cannot let her go—he won't risk losing his child! But can their marriage of convenience become a family of convenience? And is there any chance, given the hotbed of revenge, sacrifice and loss that has grown up around their relationship, that it might become something more?

I really hope you enjoy reading *THE ARRANGED BRIDES* stories as much as I enjoyed writing them. If you'd like to learn more about me or my books, visit my website at www.trishmorey.com and maybe even drop me a line at trish@trishmorey.com—I love hearing from readers.

Happy reading!

Trish x

Trish Morey is an Australian who's also spent time living and working in New Zealand and England. Now she's settled with her husband and four young daughters in a special part of South Australia surrounded by orchards and bushland, and visited by the occasional koala and kangaroo. With a life-long love of reading, she penned her first book at age eleven, after which life, career and a growing family kept her busy until once again she could indulge her desire to create characters and stories, this time in romance. Having her work published is a dream come true. Visit Trish at her website at www.trishmorey.com

Recent titles by the same author:

STOLEN BY THE SHEIKH*
THE ITALIAN BOSS'S SECRET CHILD
THE ITALIAN'S VIRGIN BRIDE
THE GREEK BOSS'S DEMAND

*Book One of *The Arranged Brides*

THE MANCINI MARRIAGE BARGAIN

BY
TRISH MOREY

MILLS & BOON®

DID YOU PURCHASE THIS BOOK WITHOUT A COVER?

If you did, you should be aware it is **stolen property** as it was reported *unsold and destroyed* by a retailer. Neither the author nor the publisher has received any payment for this book.

All the characters in this book have no existence outside the imagination of the author, and have no relation whatsoever to anyone bearing the same name or names. They are not even distantly inspired by any individual known or unknown to the author, and all the incidents are pure invention.

All Rights Reserved including the right of reproduction in whole or in part in any form. This edition is published by arrangement with Harlequin Enterprises II B.V. The text of this publication or any part thereof may not be reproduced or transmitted in any form or by any means, electronic or mechanical, including photocopying, recording, storage in an information retrieval system, or otherwise, without the written permission of the publisher.

This book is sold subject to the condition that it shall not, by way of trade or otherwise, be lent, resold, hired out or otherwise circulated without the prior consent of the publisher in any form of binding or cover other than that in which it is published and without a similar condition including this condition being imposed on the subsequent purchaser.

MILLS & BOON and MILLS & BOON with the Rose Device are registered trademarks of the publisher.

*First published in Great Britain 2005
Harlequin Mills & Boon Limited,
Eton House, 18-24 Paradise Road, Richmond, Surrey TW9 1SR*

© Trish Morey 2005

ISBN 0 263 84189 8

*Set in Times Roman 10½ on 12¼ pt.
01-1005-45191*

*Printed and bound in Spain
by Litografía Rosés, S.A., Barcelona*

CHAPTER ONE

THE noise woke her—the insistent dull pounding that crashed its way into her receding dreams and brought Helene Grainger to wakefulness in a foggy panic. One blurred glance at the red electronic display and her head momentarily flopped back onto her pillow with relief. She'd been asleep less than an hour—she wasn't late for her early morning taxi after all.

The thumping cranked up a notch and she staggered out of bed, shrugging into her silk robe and slippers, her mind clicking into gear. So if it wasn't a burly taxi driver anxious not to lose his hefty fare to Charles de Gaulle airport, who the hell would be beating their fist against her door at this time of night? *Unless Agathe from the apartment next door had had another seizure.*

Her slippered feet padded faster along the passageway. Maybe she'd fallen? Eugene wouldn't be able to lift her on his own. *'Je viens!'* she called. *I'm coming.*

Throwing security measures aside in her rush to help, she pulled open the door only to instantly recoil, her insides performing a slow roll, her mind turning cartwheels while she absorbed the frozen snapshot before her.

His fist was curled and raised ready for another blow, his eyes were wild and tormented and his dark hair mussed and troubled, as if his hand had been giving it grief until he'd taken to pounding her door with it instead. His other hand gripped white-knuckled onto some kind of leather folio.

'Paolo.' She whispered his name on a breath, aching under the weight of years of pointless longing and wasted nights. But it was cold dread that flavoured her thoughts right now. She'd always known that one day he'd come—but she'd never imagined it would be like this, that Paolo would look so strained, so intense. 'What is it?'

He sucked in a lungful of air, holding it in his broad chest as he let his fist slowly melt back into a hand and drop down to his side. A muscle in his whiskered unshaven jaw twitched, pulling up one side of his mouth into a half-smile, half-grimace as he suddenly let go the breath he'd been holding. A hint of coffee laced with whiskey, overlaid with the unmistakable essence of Paolo himself—the very taste of him curled into her senses as his agonised eyes continued to hold hers.

Then slowly, almost imperceptibly, he shook his head. 'It's over.'

The sound of locks being pulled back, of a security chain being hooked into place and a doorknob turning, all of these things leapt to centre stage in her consciousness even as Paolo's words struck a chilling void in her heart.

It's over. But why should that come as such a shock? She'd been expecting this moment for nearly half her life yet all those years of waiting, all those years of knowing, in no way diminished the pain.

Because she'd never wanted it to be over.

The door to the adjacent apartment opened on a creak, jerking to a stop against the short chain.

'Helene! Dois-j'appeler la police?' Eugene's voice croaked from behind the door, frail and betraying its owner's octogenarian status. Late-night visitors to her apartment were unheard of; no wonder he had thoughts of calling the police.

Stepping past Paolo and into the dim glow of the night-time hall lighting, she could just make out Eugene's gnarled features peering inquisitively around the door. *'Mais non, Eugene,'* she said, setting her voice to soothe. *'C'est juste un vieil ami.'*

Through the crack in the door Eugene's scowl deepened. She could almost see the cogs in his ancient mind turning—an old friend who made such a racket?

'Je suis désolée du bruit,' she said, apologising for the noise.

'Bon,' he said gruffly, as if he didn't mean it, with a last nervous sideways twitch of his eyes before retreating inside his apartment, his door closing behind him and the bolts sliding home once more.

She turned back to Paolo and their eyes collided. His dark scrutiny held such raw pain she could feel its jagged edges reaching out to scrape uncomfortably against her own feelings. Yet he was a man who would soon be free. What had happened to cause him such anguish?

'I guess you'd better come in,' she said at last, reverting to her native English, her heart thumping louder under the weight of his leaden gaze. Even Eugene's interruption couldn't stall the mounting trepidation in her body, the dread as she battled to come to terms with Paolo's spoken words.

Because this was no social call.

'I should come back tomorrow,' he said, backing away as if suddenly struck by the late hour. 'I'm disturbing your neighbours.'

'You've disturbed all of us already,' she stated plainly. 'But I'm leaving in the morning. Let's get this over with.'

Instinctively she reached for his forearm as she stepped back into the doorway, looking to draw him inside, but one touch of his arm, one hint of the tight flesh, the corded muscles hidden beneath his leather coat, and her hand jerked away.

He wasn't hers to touch.

He never had been.

A pity that hadn't stopped the thrill.

He watched her turn and lead the way into her apartment as he sucked in a breath. She seemed as strung out as he felt, though that was hardly surprising. She'd probably done her best to forget about him—to forget all about the circumstances that had brought them together in the first place.

Dio—he'd done his best to as well! And for the most part it had worked—until just lately, when their shared past had come crashing back in glorious widescreen detail.

His eyes followed her progress into the apartment. He could still walk away. Come back at a better time. Maybe even just send a fax and make the whole deal more official. He was a lawyer, for God's sake; he dealt with much bigger stuff than this unemotionally all the time.

And he almost did. But there was something about her—the crazy waves her ash-blonde hair had formed when pressed against her pillow, the shadowed eyes that hinted of secrets, the full lips plumped and pink with the scraping action of her upper teeth...

She was so much like the girl he'd known years ago, her genteel British accent unchanged, her attitude the same mixture of defiance and vulnerability, and yet he could see there was more.

He closed his eyes and called upon a mightier strength. Because the seductive sway of her hips underneath the silky robe made him forget the pain of why he was here, and made him ache for much more than anything to which he was entitled.

With a sigh he followed her into the apartment, unable to pull his eyes from her retreating form even if he'd wanted to.

Had Helene been so beguiling twelve years ago? Had their problems back then been so paramount that he'd simply never noticed, or was it just that time had transformed a pretty young student into a stunning woman?

With a struggle his mind clicked back into logic mode. It was academic really—it was a bit late to start noticing how good-looking a woman was a mere ten minutes before you divorced her.

She turned and waited for him in her tastefully decorated reception room, switching on a low leadlight table lamp in deference to the late hour, the coloured glass segments of the shade casting a soft, comfortable glow over the room. The truth was stark enough without illuminating it in the glare of one hundred watts.

'Can I get you a drink?'

He definitely looked as if he needed one, but that wasn't the only reason she'd asked. Right now she needed space to breathe. Because no matter that she'd anticipated this moment for twelve long years it was still too sudden, too unwanted, too damned painful.

It was time to get rid of her.

She concentrated on keeping her breathing calm, on keeping her hands from tangling with each other as she awaited his response. He seemed to fill the space in the modest-sized room, making the furniture look too small. He warmed the air around her until her face felt bright and flushed. He made her wish she had a whole lot more on under this robe than one tiny pair of pink cotton panties.

He seemed to think about her question for a while and then, 'Coffee?'

With relief she darted for the kitchen. If the silence between them had stretched out any longer, something would have snapped—probably her. She flicked on the kettle, piled the grounds into the plunger, tinkering with cups, but her mind refused to focus on simply making coffee.

Twelve years had seen the lean, good-looking student turn into a man who looked as if he could have been carved from stone. Even sporting a late-o'clock shadow, troubled eyes and mussed hair Paolo looked good. Better than good, and in fact better even than the pictures of him she'd pored over from time to time when she'd stumbled upon them in her hairdresser's magazines. Somehow in those he'd always seemed to be glaring at the photographer, as if resentful of being captured on film.

The woman on his arm had been less camera-shy, smiling radiantly as they had been captured on film. But who could blame her for looking so happy? She had it all. A successful designer for the Milan-based fashion house of Bacelli, she was simply stunning, and she had Paolo.

Sapphire Clemenger.

There was no way Helene could forget her name. The woman-in-waiting, the imminent Mrs Paolo Mancini, according to the social pages. Well, if Paolo's sudden visit was any indication, it looked as if she was about to get her opportunity. Paolo obviously couldn't wait to be free so they could tie the knot.

'You don't seem very happy to see me.'

Her spine stiffened and she took the time to draw in a fortifying breath, depressing the plunger before she turned. He was standing in the doorway, one arm resting up against the jamb. He'd taken off his coat and the white shirt fitted without clinging, showing off the width of his chest and the long, lean line of his body. Her mouth went dry.

'It's late,' she said on a swallow. 'I thought something had happened to Agathe next door; she's got a bad heart. I was worried about her and Eugene. They know to call me if anything happens...'

Her rambling words trailed off, evaporated, in the heat from his gaze.

'You must know why I'm here.'

She nodded, fighting her shoulders' determination to sag. She couldn't show him how much she was affected by this. 'Khaled's married, then.'

'Yes.'

The word sliced through her heart.

Knowledge wasn't power.

Knowledge was pain.

Yet it was crazy. She should be happy to escape from the shadows of Khaled Al-Ateeq, the man she'd been promised to when barely seventeen, brokered as part of a deal with Khaled's father to further her own father's oil interests in the Middle East, and the man she'd enraged by running off with Paolo and marrying him first.

Their short, civil ceremony had sounded the death knell for the arranged marriage and for the deal. And still she'd been so terrified that Khaled might persist in his attempts to come after her that Paolo had vowed to stay married to her until Khaled had taken another wife.

It had been such a simple plan—foolproof—and neither of them had thought Khaled would take longer than a year or two to find a new wife.

Instead, for more than a decade the threat of retribution had loomed long and large over their lives, a permanent and poisoned cloud that had threatened to snuff out any and all relationships she'd had with men and any chance that Paolo had had to start a real family of his own.

Until now.

Now that Khaled was married they were both free.

Except that, for her, freedom meant severing the very tie she had with the only man she'd ever wanted.

'He certainly took his time about it.'

A muscled worked in his jaw. Something fleeting skidded across his eyes and she realised her attempt to lighten the mood had fallen flat.

'You don't have to be worried about him any more. You're safe. He'll never trouble you again.'

Emotion hitched in his words, forcing her to really look at him, and guilt speared her deep inside. For twelve years he'd stuck by his promise to her. He could have been married already with a houseful of children. He should have been! Instead he'd been lumbered with a wife he'd never wanted and a promise he'd had no idea would be so binding.

No wonder he wanted out.

'So you've brought me some papers to sign?' she asked, pushing past with the tray, trying not to breathe in as she moved past him, trying not to breathe in the scent she'd so quickly have to forget all over again.

He nodded in the direction of the sitting room. 'They're in the folio.'

'Then let's get started,' she said brightly, trying to infuse her words with something more closely resembling enthusiasm.

He pulled out the documents while she poured the coffee, all the while wondering why she hadn't had the sense to make herself a cup of herbal tea instead. It was late and she needed to get some sleep before her early morning flight. The last thing she wanted after tonight's visitor was a caffeine-induced think-fest.

Then she took one look at Paolo and realised she was kidding herself. Whatever she drank tonight there was no hope of getting any sleep. Not now. Not knowing it had all come to an end at last.

He sat down alongside her on the settee, brushing the long length of his upper leg against hers and inadvertently snaring one side of the fabric of her robe.

Too late she realised what was happening. By the time she'd shifted herself away, one side of the slippery fabric was well and truly wedged under his thigh, totally exposing her left leg from her knee all the way past her too-brief panties.

She grasped the other side of the robe and pulled it over before the gap could expose more of her midriff than it already did, instantly regretting her decision not to have taken the opportunity while she'd had it to put more layers of clothing between her and Paolo. But given that she normally slept naked, it was lucky she had anything on at all underneath her robe.

Luck was hardly what she was feeling right now, though, as a combination of exposure to the cool air and a major dose of embarrassment turned her skin to goose-bumps.

He seemed to take an inordinately long time to register her distress, although it could very well have taken the space of one hitched breath as her whole world ground to a halt. His eyes shifted from the papers he was holding to her knee and then all too slowly drifted up, way up. He blinked, dangerously slowly, when his eyes reached where the skin disappeared under her robe. Then his eyes moved to where her hands gripped white-knuckled at her waist-tie, and finally to her face, although she was sure there was just a moment there where they'd hesitated, without a doubt registering the points of her nipples, straining firm and insistent against the perilously thin fabric.

His jaw tightened and something flared in his eyes, something hot and dangerous and powerfully magnetic. Blood pulsed in secret places as his heated gaze turned her embarrassment into something much, much more primal. Then, almost as quickly, his eyes cooled to apology mode. A second later he was out of his seat and across the room from her, feigning sudden interest in the items on her mantelpiece.

'I'm sorry,' he said, his voice sounding unusually thick.

She covered herself, tucking the newly freed fabric securely around her while her skin burned with mortification.

Oh, she'd seen that look before; she'd heard those very words from his mouth. Surely he hadn't thought she'd been trying to seduce him again? She was no naïve seventeen-year-old on her wedding night. She wasn't stupid enough to try that again.

Her memory vividly played back his words, still startlingly fresh despite the weight of the intervening years. *'I'm sorry,'* he'd told her back then, unwinding her arms from where she'd wrapped them around his neck, *'But this marriage isn't about sex.'*

He couldn't possibly think she'd want to bring that humiliation upon herself again? He hadn't wanted her on their wedding night and he'd just made it doubly plain that he didn't want her now. Why the hell would he when finally he had his chance to be rid of her for ever? Did he really think she still cared enough to try, even after twelve years of nothing more than an occasional Christmas card from his law office?

He'd be crazy to think it.

Totally crazy.

Except that she did.

Time and pain hadn't erased the attraction at all. If anything they'd honed it, sharpened it to such a fine point that when she'd opened the door tonight it had felt like a needle exploding in her heart, its fragments burying themselves deep into her flesh like tiny splinters.

Damn, but how could a man you'd promised yourself years ago that you'd forget still manage to turn you to pulp? It was hardly fair. Especially when all he wanted was to be free to marry someone else.

Then again, if he deserved anything after being faithful to his promise for so long, it was a rapid release from the ties that bound them together. At the very least she owed him that.

'No apology required,' she said quietly into the low-lit room as he continued to study the objects and the few photographs on her mantelpiece. 'I'm sure you're in a hurry to get going.' *To get married.* 'Give me the papers to sign while you have your coffee.'

He could sure do with coffee. Or something stronger. But at least now he could turn around safely without her thinking he'd come here tonight to get a whole lot more than just her signature.

It had been a long time since he'd had a woman. Months. But he hadn't realised how long until his need had threatened to spin out of control just then.

And the last twelve years had shaped Helene into a very desirable woman indeed. Her greenish eyes flickered with gold in the lamplight and spoke of both intelligence and warmth; her chin might be firmly angled like her father's, yet her lips were full and inviting. And as he dipped lower to place the papers in front of her even the faint remnants of her chosen fragrance melded with her own natural scent, making something new, something utterly feminine and alluring.

She was one attractive woman all right. But it had been the sight of all that creamy skin on a leg that seemed to go forever coupled with the knowledge that she couldn't be wearing a whole lot more than a tiny pair of pink pants under that robe that had made him suddenly wish he could tumble her straight back into the bed his late-night visit had pulled her from.

Or maybe she hadn't been alone.

All of a sudden he wanted to know more about her. What had she been doing for the last twelve years? Who had she been with?

And was someone waiting in bed for her even now?

A glance at her photographs revealed nothing. There was no evidence of anyone else in the apartment, no trace of masculine input into the soft decor, but still he burned to know.

'The places where you need to sign are flagged,' he offered. 'Are you sure I'm not disturbing anyone else by being here this late? A flatmate? A boyfriend?'

Her eyes snapped from the papers straight up to his. 'Perfectly sure,' she replied coolly.

He cursed inwardly. It wasn't the answer he wanted. It told him nothing more than he already knew.

'So you don't have a boyfriend, or he doesn't live here?'

She put the pen down and looked up at him again through narrowed eyes. 'I didn't realise that's what you were asking. For what it's worth there's no boyfriend, live-in or live-out. There's also no flatmate. Obviously I don't have a husband, except you of course. The sooner you let me sign these papers, though, the sooner I'll have that sorted.'

'I would have thought they'd be queuing at the door,' he said through barely separated lips, resuming his investigation of her room, leaving her to study the papers. Was she that desperate to sign?

His eyes fell on an old photograph of a couple he recognised instantly. Her parents. *His parents-in-law.* Caroline Grainger was smiling into the camera, looking every bit the society wife, smiling benignly in her neat-trimmed jacket and pearls, her hair immaculate, while Richard Grainger's cold blue eyes gazed smugly at the camera as if he owned the world. Given his business interests all over the globe, he just about did.

'How are your parents?' he asked, over his shoulder.

'I don't know,' she said.

He put the picture down and turned to face her. He sensed a note in there that suggested things weren't at all right. 'You don't know?'

She dropped the pen on the table and took a deep breath, running her hands back through her hair. Fascinated, he watched the way it straightened out long under her fingers only to bounce back into its shoulder-length waves. He liked the way her hand could bury itself in its thick depths. It was the kind of hair you could lose yourself in.

'The last time I heard from my father,' she said, pulling his focus back onto her words, 'was four weeks after our wedding. You'd returned to Milan by then and I'd just found my first flat in Paris. That's where his solicitor's letter finally caught up with me. In it he told me he considered he'd never had a daughter and that I'd never speak to either of them again.'

'He disowned you?'

'That's about the size of it.'

'I never knew.'

She shrugged. 'I expected him to be angry. We'd blown his deal sky-high. He'd not only lost face, he'd lost millions—potentially billions if the venture had been the success they expected. He wasn't about to let me get off easily after that. He wanted me to pay.'

'But to cut you off like that—and from your mother.'

'It's okay really,' she said, much too quickly for him to believe it was. 'I got what I wanted after all. I have a good career with the International Bureau for Women and I've made a good life here in Paris.' She smiled weakly up at him. 'To think I owe it all to you.'

'No,' he said. 'You've made your life a success all by yourself.'

'But I would never have had the opportunity without you. Nobody else cared enough to stop what was going on and, even if they had, the prospect of acting in defiance of my father would have turned them to jelly. You were the only person who cared enough to stand up for me, who wouldn't let me be traded off as just another piece of merchandise in my father's bizarre business deal.'

He wasn't sure his actions had been all that noble. He'd been enraged that a fellow student, a good friend, could be placed in such a position by her family, and with the impetuosity of youth and the certainty that they were wrong he'd been determined that their plan to sell off their daughter would be foiled. And he and Helene had simply found a way to do it.

He took a deep breath. Looking back, knowing what he knew now, knowing what he had set in train, maybe he should never have got involved. Maybe he should have turned his back on her and let her marry Khaled.

'Don't you understand,' she continued, 'that you gave me my freedom at the cost of your own? I know I can never repay you for the years you wasted being tied to me, but you have to know that I will always, always be grateful for what you have done.'

She smiled again, belying the moisture filming her eyes, and something pulled tight inside him. How could he have abandoned her? How could he have even considered that he might have? It was all he could do to stand in one spot and not rush over to collect her into her arms and kiss her pain away.

But he dared not do it. Once already he'd come close to losing control. If he kissed her, there'd be no way he'd want to stop, because he knew without a doubt that it would help erase his own pain.

Instead he forced a smile to his own lips and tried not to think about the devastating consequences of something they had both done so long ago, tried not to think about another woman, now tied to the very same man he'd saved Helene from.

So what that he'd saved Helene? He'd done nothing to save Sapphy from the same fate. He'd as good as delivered her to Khaled on a platter. He had little to feel proud of.

He needed to close this conversation down. It was getting too dangerous, too close to the bone. 'It was the least I could do,' he said, his voice a dry rasp as he turned back to her small collection of photographs before she detected anything was wrong. A few seconds later the sounds of pages turning told him she'd directed her attentions back onto the documents.

He let go a breath he hadn't realised he'd been holding. Coming tonight had been a mad idea. He should have sent the papers. Coming here was like ripping off a bandage on a wound that had never healed and that now lay exposed, raw and weeping and edged with decay.

'There's something I don't understand,' she said after a little while, interrupting his thoughts. 'These are papers for what looks like a regular divorce. Only I thought—'

He looked around and waited, watching the colour in her cheeks rising. Then, when it was clear she wasn't going to go on, asked, 'You thought what?'

'Well, I just had it in mind that we would be seeking an annulment. You know, given…'

Again she trailed off and he took a step closer, watching the turmoil of emotions flashing through her eyes.

'Given that we never actually consummated the marriage?'

She nodded, her exposed skin colouring brighter by the second. Her chin kicked up on a swallow and he followed the movement in her throat, watching it disappear into the spot where her skin dipped into the hollow just above her collar-bone.

Such smooth skin, fair and creamy all the way to where it disappeared behind the V of her robe. All the way down and all the way up, if what he'd seen before was any indication. He swallowed, amazed that they'd never taken that one extra step to consummate their marriage.

She'd wanted to, he remembered. After the tension of carrying out their plan, after he'd successfully whisked her away from her mother while on a London shopping trip and kept her hidden until he'd slipped a ring on her finger, they'd both been on a high. They'd outsmarted both her domineering family and the heir to an independent Arab state, they'd foiled Richard Grainger's attempt to sell off his daughter to the highest bidder, and they'd managed to get away with it.

After dispatching copies of the photographic evidence and the marriage certificate to her family, they'd celebrated in true student style in a friend's shabby bedsit with a bottle of cheap fizz, congratulating themselves on how clever they were and laughing and dancing into the night.

And then she'd kissed him and suggested they go to bed together and suddenly everything had become a whole lot more complicated...

He could easily have made love to her that night. Very easily. But he hadn't wanted to take advantage of her while she'd been high on their success and cheap wine. And he hadn't wanted her to think he was expecting her to pay him back in sex. He remembered he'd tried to explain and made a mess of it, but she'd made no further attempts to get physical, so no doubt she must have been relieved he hadn't taken her up on the offer. He had been at the time too, although now he wasn't so sure.

It was clear to Helene he hadn't forgotten either. She could just about see the frame-by-frame action replaying on the screen of his dark chocolate eyes. What an idiot she'd been back then, and how incredibly stupid of her to bring it up again now. It was bad enough thinking back on the humiliating experience herself without reminding Paolo of her embarrassment.

He suddenly shook his head, as if trying to rid himself of the images. 'In legal terms, it's not actually relevant. It's a common misconception, but lack of consummation isn't usually sufficient grounds for annulment.'

Not relevant? Her mind reeled as her perspective on the past shifted. She'd imagined he'd turned her down that night because making love might have hurt their chances of escaping the marriage. It might have damaged their right to an annulment. But, from what Paolo was saying, that had never been an option. Which meant he'd turned her down because he hadn't wanted to make love to her at all.

What a total fool she'd been all these years!

'Our cause,' he said, his voice breaking into her thoughts, 'is separation for at least two years with mutual consent.'

She clenched the pen, her fingers tight and stiff. Just sign the papers, she told herself, doing her best to suppress the stinging sensation behind her eyes. Sign the papers and let him go.

Because he was never yours to begin with.

Without bothering to read the small print, she turned up the first page flagged for her signature and scrawled off her name.

'Aren't you going to read it first?'

'I've read enough,' she said, her throat oppressively tight. 'Besides, you're a lawyer, I assume you know what you're doing.'

Something in her voice alerted him and he took a step closer to the coffee-table.

'Helene?'

She looked up briefly and he saw the moisture pooling in her eyes. She was crying?

'What?'

'I thought you'd be happy about this—about Khaled getting married at last.'

'Of course, I'm happy,' she said, reeling off another crazy looped signature, another nail in the lid of the coffin of their marriage. She swiped at her eyes with her pen hand when she was done. 'It's wonderful news. You must be relieved yourself.'

Ignoring his own advice to himself, he sat down nearby and placed one hand under her chin, gently directing her to face him. 'Then why are you crying?'

'Happy tears,' she said, twisting her lips into a wonky smile as she pulled her chin away. 'It's great news really. So who's the poor bride? Anyone we know?'

His swift intake of air pulled her straight back out of the documents.

'What's wrong?'

His eyes swirled with pain, the flesh of his face

pinched and tightened, and instantly she knew that this was no accidental marriage. 'Who is she?'

His eyes stared back at her, but she could tell they saw nothing. They were blank, empty shells, his thoughts obviously centred on somewhere else— *someone* else—and her blood ran cold with fear.

'Khaled promised he would take his revenge upon me. He warned me that one day he would steal someone close to me, steal them away from me, as I had done to him.' His eyes changed and she knew he'd brought her back into focus. 'Just as your father wanted you to pay, Khaled could not let me go.'

'Oh, no!' she said, one hand pressed against her mouth.

'And he did. He took someone I care deeply for. Just as he'd promised. Just as he'd sworn.'

His words snagged and he stopped, hauling in a breath. She waited in dread for him to go on, witnessing the turmoil in his eyes, sensing the devastation of his pain.

'And he married her?' she asked with disbelief.

He smiled, but it wasn't with joy or elation. It was a smile empty of any emotions, a hollow smile that spoke of his loss.

'Oh, yes. He married her.'

'Who is she?' Her voice was no more than a whisper, her dread a living thing, threatening to strangle her words.

'I don't know if you ever heard of her. She is—or rather was—a fashion designer for the House of Bacelli in Milan. Her name is Sapphy—Sapphire Clemenger.'

CHAPTER TWO

'OH, MY God! No, Paolo… Not Sapphire! I heard—I thought—-oh, my God!'

Helene burst out of the settee, arms wrapped tightly around herself, shaking her head, trying to come to grips with the disaster that she'd caused, the anguish that she alone was responsible for. Unable to stand still, she paced the carpet, unable to stop, unable to rest with the knowledge of what she'd done.

Paolo's late-night visit, his stressed-out state, the pounding on the door—suddenly it all made sense. This was a man in mourning. A man bereft. And she was to blame.

'This is all my fault!'

'Helene. Don't think that.'

'But it is. All of it is down to me. Down to what I wanted. Don't you see?' She turned to face him, throwing her hands out wide. 'If you hadn't married me back then, none of this would have happened.'

'And what was the alternative?' He was up now, his voice raised, his eyes blazing. 'Marry Khaled? That was never an alternative and you know it.'

'But look what's happened because of it. It's been like a dark threat hanging over our lives for twelve long years. And now just look at what it's done to your life and to Sapphire's! It's too high a price to pay. I never should have asked it of you. I had no right.'

The weight of all the things she'd cost him bore heavily down upon her—twelve years of his life ripped away, twelve years of being unable to commit to a relationship, twelve years of being denied the chance to start a family. And as if that weren't enough, now she'd cost him the woman he'd wanted for his wife.

It was too much!

She sucked in a shuddering breath as she covered her mouth with her hands. 'I'm sorry, Paolo. I'm so very, very sorry.'

Then she couldn't speak any more as the sobs overtook her, great heaving sobs that racked her chest, doubling her over with the pain of knowing what his promise to her had cost him.

She was barely aware that he'd touched her, but then he was straightening her up and pulling her in close to him. Gratefully she collapsed against his chest, tangling her fists in his shirt as his arms wound around her, while the tears continued to fall, the sobs unrelenting.

'Let it go,' he said softly. 'Let it all out.'

She had no choice. She had no energy to fight it. It was all coming out anyway, a torrent of emotion that had been walled up all this time, buried away, deep inside.

Once again she felt her shock at the callousness of her father when he'd coldly informed her of his decision to trade her off. She felt the despair when her mother had ignored her pleas for help and she relived the fear and desperation that had driven her to find any solution, anything that would save her from her fate.

She cried with the relief she'd felt when Paolo had come up with his crazy plan, the answer to her prayers. He'd done more than offer her a lifeline. He'd literally saved her life when it had seemed that the only way out of her predicament was to throw hers away.

And her tears mourned for Paolo and for the life he should have had, the life now denied to him for ever.

Her breathing was still nowhere near normal when she noticed the rocking. Paolo's arms were locked around her, his chin resting against her head, and he was swaying, gently moving from side to side, an age-old soothing motion. It felt good. Paolo felt good.

His shirt was wet through under her face, but it was far from uncomfortable. Instead the steady pounding of his heartbeat, the warm, musky scent of skin made her want to bury her face deeper into him. She could taste him in her breath. She could feel his strength feeding into hers, calming her ragged sighs.

And yet she didn't belong here, in Paolo's arms. She needed to sign the papers and let him get out of here and get on with his life. Reluctantly she lifted her head from his chest. Her eyes fixed on his shirt, she drew the back of one hand across her cheeks, but she knew there was little point trying to look presentable. She looked up and saw it then, the moisture filming his own eyes. And then he blinked and it was almost gone, except for the dampness clinging to his long lashes, making them shine glossy and thick.

'Oh, Paolo,' she uttered on a breath, her heart breaking even more, knowing that she was the one responsible for his tears. 'I'm so sorry—for everything.'

He loosened one arm and for a moment she thought he was going to let her go completely, but one hand splayed in the centre of her back, keeping her close, as his other found her chin, tilting it up towards him.

'Enough with the apologies.'

'But, Paolo—'

'Enough.' He touched his finger to her lips to shush her, his eyes narrowing as he looked down, while the heat inside them cranked up.

It was contagious. Like a pilot light suddenly given a flow of fuel, something flared into life inside her, coursing through her and warming everywhere it touched.

And everywhere she touched him.

Heat gathered and pooled in low places as every point of their contact became more significant. Her breasts felt swollen and full, her nipples hard even as they butted into his chest, her thighs wedged tight against his.

Something had changed. No longer was he merely someone holding her, soothing her. He was a man, all man, and a man whose body was showing unmistakable signs of arousal.

Her heart stopped. Or was it just her breath? Whatever, it seemed the whole world was waiting for something to happen.

And then his mouth was on hers and she didn't need to breathe, didn't even need to think. She had everything she needed and more in his sweet kiss. Softly, tenderly, his lips brushed against hers, the supple warmth of his mouth like a salve to her hurt, the rasp of his chin like a gentle file scraping away her pain.

Her hands untangled themselves from the knots they'd formed in his shirt as her body relaxed into his, and her fingers flexed against the fine fabric, exploring, learning, drinking in the feel of the firm, muscled flesh beneath.

His kiss deepened in response, demanding more of her and taking more. Much more. The taste of him filled her, fuelled her, obliterating every last trace of logic from her mind.

Why was he here after all this time? Why had he come? She didn't really care. Because warm breath was skidding across her cheek, heavily laced with the taste of their kiss and the scent of desire, and that was all that mattered.

Heat followed the course of his hands, transmitting through the thin silk of her robe as if it wasn't there. And then his mouth was at her throat, setting off new fires under her skin and making her hungry—hungry for him.

His hand pulled back the side of her robe and his mouth followed the movement, tracing the line of her collar-bone to her shoulder. She shuddered against him, her spine melting, every part of her skin looking to be the next place in line under his hot mouth.

He returned to her lips before trailing kisses down the other side, pulling away that side of her robe in his quest. She clung to his back, relying on him to keep her upright, knowing that her knees couldn't support her while she concentrated on the magic from his mouth.

Then his lips were at her breast, on her breast, his

tongue rolling around the hard bud, and sensation speared through her, setting off a desperate need deep inside. Tissues tingled, moisture welled as her body prepared to open itself to him.

He lifted his mouth away, his eyes fixed on the fabric, now moulded to the firm nub of her nipple. A low rumble, like a growl melded with passion, emanated from his throat and his eyes flicked up to hers.

Hunger filled their dark depths. Hunger and need. She was afraid to let her eyes slide away in case she missed something, but even so she was afraid to hold them, in case he might read too much in hers.

Whatever he saw, it gave him what he was looking for. He tugged one end of the looped tie at her waist. She sucked in a breath as the tie fell undone and the sides of her robe slid slowly apart.

Breath hissed through his teeth, his eyes glowing in frank appreciation as he drank in her near nakedness. Her breasts seemed to swell even harder in response, the points of her nipples achingly taut as anticipation built to fever pitch inside her.

'Perfezione,' he said, resorting to his native tongue on a breath that sounded almost like worship.

And then things sped up. His arms swept around her, dislodging the robe hanging from her shoulders. The fabric pooled behind her, but there was no time to mourn its loss, not with Paolo's mouth on hers, his hands exploring every dip and curve of her skin, his arousal a pressing imperative between them.

She pushed herself against him, need driving her to force her hips ever closer. His hands skimmed her back, tucking under the band on her panties and capturing her naked flesh, wedging her neatly between his pressing hands and the grinding force of his own desire.

His mouth dipped to her throat and she gasped for air, but the oxygen was consumed more rapidly than she could suck it in, burning white hot in the heat of their passion. Each breath, each second burned the flames higher, the need greater.

The need to touch his skin.

The need to feel his skin against hers.

The need to have him inside her.

It was all-consuming. And she wanted to be consumed. She wanted him, deep inside her. Only that could quell this desperate, mounting ache.

Frantically she scrabbled for the buttons of his shirt, not caring whether they came undone or flew off in her quest to get at his body, while his kisses continued their way down towards her breasts. She pulled the shirt open and her hands revelled in the satiny touch of his skin, the well-defined muscles below, in the contrast of the springy hairs that swirled between his pebble-hard nipples.

Her hands followed the line of his muscled chest down, over an abdomen that tightened deliciously under her touch as he caught his breath. She reached the band on his trousers, slipping the pads of her fingers beneath. Steel bands trapped her wrists and his mouth nuzzled her ear.

'Have mercy,' he said, his voice rough and edgy. 'It's been a while.'

He had to be kidding. It had been for ever. Or that was how it seemed. Two boyfriends in twelve years. Two unsatisfactory love affairs that had left her thinking she had some kind of problem. Maybe she did.

Certainly neither man had made her feel a fraction of what she was feeling right now. Neither had ever come close to setting her alight. Right now she couldn't even remember their names.

And he wanted mercy?

She curved one hand out of his grasp, turning it palm down against the straining fabric, her fingers instinctively tightening around the rigid proof of his desire.

'Not a chance,' she whispered.

His mouth and body stilled and for a cold, hard moment she thought she'd blown it and gone too far, and her spirits plummeted. She'd never tried a move so bold and outrageous before because she'd never before felt so driven, so motivated by need. But maybe she just wasn't cut out for coming the temptress.

And then he groaned, a low guttural sound, a warning of things to come, and expectation resumed its heady build-up through her veins.

He drew her back into his arms and carried her through to her bedroom, placing her with almost reverential awe on her bed. In almost the same next movement he'd shrugged off his shirt and shoes. She didn't have a chance to feel overdressed because in a moment his pants were similarly dispensed with, her pink panties meeting the same fate.

His eyes drank her in.

'So beautiful, *bella donna*,' he said, lying alongside her. Then his lips found her again.

His liquid voice and his generous words fed into her senses. The passion in his eyes set her extremities alight.

And his mouth…

Oh, his hot mouth made magic on her skin, casting spells with his lips, weaving charms with his tongue. It was witchcraft, seduction by sorcery, pure enchantment, and she was completely and utterly bewitched.

It was all she could do to cling to him as his hands made complementary havoc elsewhere. Everywhere they touched produced sparks and fireworks, but none so much as when his fingers lingered over the spring of her curls.

Breath caught in her chest as his fingers dipped lower, slipping amidst her most intimate place with an apparent knowingness that felt so right.

Hot kisses returned to her mouth and she let herself open to his fiery onslaught. Then she heard his breath catch on a groan and he shifted over her. She felt his weight pressing between her legs and the insistent column of his erection between them.

'I want you,' he said, his eyes burning with need, and she almost believed him. But then amidst the desire she also saw the clouds scudding across their surface, as if he were doing battle with demons.

It hit her like a blow to the chest. *Sapphire! He's seeing Sapphire. He's thinking she should be the one he is with.*

And there was nothing left for her but to try and help him forget. Maybe just for a little while she could help dull the pain of his loss.

She closed her eyes as she felt him pressing up against her. So hard and yet so warm. So smooth and yet so powerful. Muscles spasmed in reaction to his touch, as if by their invitation they could draw him in. He leaned further over, drinking in her mouth with his, plundering with his tongue and then meeting her need with one long thrust that made her arch her back and threw her reeling from the kiss.

Slowly he withdrew, only to fill her again, lunging himself to the hilt.

She matched his movements, tilting her hips to receive him, tightening around him to prolong the pleasure, working in with the rhythm he established. She wanted to give him pleasure, to make him forget, to pay him back something of the loss she had caused him, but it was building, her own feelings escalating into something potent, something dangerously close to boiling over.

And there was nothing at all she could do about it. Then his mouth moved to her breast, his teeth tugging on the tight peak, his tongue curling and cajoling, and it happened.

She felt herself come in high-definition colours, colours that shattered and fragmented into a million tiny shards that hovered in the air like sparkling fireflies. His own release prolonged her own, so that wave after wave of shuddering sensations followed, throwing up more clouds of the shimmering lights, glistening and sparkling and eventually fading like spent fireworks as her body slowly came back to earth.

They collapsed together amongst the pillows, breathing deep, the scent of their lovemaking a blanket to warm them. She must have dozed off, when a sound, his voice, brought her to.

'Did you say something?' she murmured.

'I said I'm sorry.'

Her warm feelings turned decidedly chilly. 'You don't need to be sorry. I believe I was a willing partner.'

He shook his head where it rested against her shoulder. 'I didn't use protection. That's never happened before.'

His words were a harsh dose of reality. What the hell had they been thinking? Except obviously they hadn't been thinking, not beyond the frantic desperation of their coupling.

'Is there reason for me to be worried?' she ventured. 'I can guarantee you're at no risk from me.'

'It's not just that,' he said. 'The last thing we both need is a baby, especially since we're about to become divorced.'

'Oh, of course.' The divorce. Her teeth dragged across her bottom lip, now plump and tender from his passionate ministrations. Of course the divorce would be uppermost in his mind. Naturally after twelve years he was looking to destroy the links that tied them together. Not forge new ones.

That's what had brought him here after all. Tonight's lovemaking was simply something that had happened between two consenting adults. It wasn't as if she meant anything to him.

'Do you take some form of contraception?'

She started to say yes, but then she remembered. She *had* been on the pill, had been on it for years to battle irregular and crampy periods. Until last month when her doctor had recommended she take a break. But she couldn't get pregnant. People tried for months after going off the pill to have a baby, didn't they? Besides, it was much too late in her cycle. She was due any day.

'I'm safe,' she said, as certain as she could be.

He pulled her to him and kissed her gently. 'Not to mention beautiful.'

The constant hum of jet engines was neither soothing enough to let her sleep, nor loud enough to drown out the memories. And she wanted to sleep. She was tired and aching and desperately, desperately running on empty. Instead she was reliving last night's lovemaking, over and over, replaying the scenes in her head, feeling the shadow of the sensations he'd awakened in her.

How many times had they made love last night? She'd lost count together with her sleep.

Thankfully he hadn't stirred when she'd left, because she had no idea what she would have said to him this morning anyway. It had been easier to write a note—although even that had taken her half a dozen attempts before she'd been satisfied. What did you say to someone you'd just made the most amazing love to all night and whom you were never likely to see again—happy divorce?

And without a doubt he'd be relieved he didn't have to worry about any awkward morning-after scenes too. She'd made sure she'd signed the papers before she'd left so he'd have nothing to complain about. He'd got what he'd come for and then some.

As for her?

She sighed, finding it impossible to get comfortable

in spite of the wide business-class seat. She'd had the night of her life. She had memories—bittersweet memories that would live in her heart for ever. Memories of a night when for just a few hours she'd been able to pretend that there was more to her relationship with Paolo than a cold, contractual arrangement—a contractual arrangement now as good as dead.

And put to death by her own hand. She'd checked and double-checked to ensure she hadn't missed a signature. She didn't want to cause him any more grief than she already had.

Because Paolo was right. It was over.

She was gone. Her side of the bed was cold, no hint of her body warmth anywhere when finally he stirred, the apartment strangely quiet. The door to the *en suite* was open, the light off. There were no sounds or smells from the kitchen, no radio or television to cover the muted traffic noise from outside.

He picked up his watch and looked disbelievingly at the hands. It was almost afternoon. He must have slept for hours when they'd finally fallen asleep. He couldn't remember sleeping this solidly in months.

But where was she? His mind searched for a clue, trying to play back their conversation from last night. But actions spoke louder than words and visions of Helene, naked and coming apart in his arms, interfered with his thought processes. She'd been so responsive, so soft and giving of herself.

After they'd made love he'd carried her into the shower and they'd washed each other and it had been another voyage of discovery. The water cascading over them both, streaming over her skin, forming rivulets down her breasts, tiny waterfalls spinning down off her nipples, his mouth lapping the tiny stream away.

And her mouth, setting his skin alight once more, building fires and need until their bodies had merged once again in their liquid world.

'Dio!' he swore as the pictures stirred his masculine response into life once more. He didn't need this right now!

The scene in the hallway gradually drifted uppermost in his mind. Hadn't she said something about leaving today? But where?

She couldn't be gone. Surely she would have said goodbye?

He called her name, waiting for a response in her soft tones, but there was none. Nothing but the womanly scent of her still lingering in the sheets, the fragrant trace of her hair on her pillow.

There was something else too. He raised himself up onto one elbow and reached over. The papers, he realised, as something small fluttered off the top and over the side of the bed. He ignored it for a moment as he leafed through the pages. She'd signed everywhere indicated and then left the papers where he had no chance to miss them.

Something inside him snapped.

Last night he'd got the impression she was almost saddened at the prospect of their phony marriage coming to a conclusion. She'd made love like a goddess, letting him worship her and giving her sweet body to him in return. And yet by her actions this morning she'd shown herself to be another person from the woman he'd met last night. To leave this way after what they'd shared—he hadn't given her credit for being so coldly calculating.

The papers could have waited. There was no real rush now, not from his perspective. It wouldn't have mattered if the papers hadn't been signed until her return from wherever it was she was going. She could have had more time to go through them, ensuring the arrangement was as they'd agreed all those years ago.

But she'd taken no time. She'd asked for none. She'd completed the papers and left them where her intention was unmistakable.

She couldn't wait to be free of him.

He threw himself out of the bed, noticing again the scrap of note paper, now on the floor, and he reached down to snatch it up, his spirits rising. So she had left him a note after all? Maybe a phone number where she could be contacted wherever she'd gone. There was no reason why they shouldn't remain friends.

Her tight, looping script stared back at him as he took in the message, his anger building more with what wasn't said than what was.

Paolo,
Help yourself to whatever you need. Let yourself out—the cleaner is coming at one.
Helene

That was it? Breath rushed out of him as if he'd been sucker punched. She didn't want him to know where she was. She obviously didn't want him to contact her. And she didn't want her cleaner to find him still here.

He screwed up the note, tossing it into the corner of the room. *Let the cleaner find that!*

He was out of here.

CHAPTER THREE

THE physician had such compassionate eyes, making it much easier to feel comfortable with him than Helene had expected. He was older than her own doctor back in Paris, maybe sixty or so, his skin ruddy in places, his jowls just starting to slip from his cheekbones, and yet his eyes were the kindest, most reassuring blue.

He'd waited outside while she'd dressed and he smiled now as he sat back down again behind his desk, making her wonder why on earth it had taken her so long to make an appointment to see someone. Sure, her three-month secondment to the New York office was nearly over and she'd be back in Paris again in two more weeks, but she'd put up with this situation for too long already and it was starting to affect her job.

The sooner she got another prescription for the pill, the sooner she'd be back to normal. Already she'd missed work on a couple of occasions, and had been tempted to take more sick leave because of the cramping and general malaise. For someone who'd only ever taken time out for rare dental appointments it was too much. She'd had enough of the discomfort and the irregular periods.

The doctor picked up a pair of glasses from the desk and without unfolding them, lifted the lenses briefly to his eyes to look down at his notes. 'Miss

Grainger,' he said, turning his attention back to her. 'How long before you're due to return to France?'

'Two weeks.' Disappointment welled as she anticipated where his line of questioning was going. Maybe she'd wasted her time coming after all. 'Surely you're not saying I should wait until I get home to get a new prescription?'

He shook his head, 'No. Merely that we've got a bit of time in that case, so I think it might pay for you to have a couple of tests before you leave for home.'

'Why? Whatever for?'

He held up one hand to quell her reaction, his eyes crinkling with compassion again. 'Nothing serious, but I think for your own peace of mind you might want to have them done as soon as possible.'

'I don't understand.'

He smiled across at her, pinching the bridge of his nose with his fingers. 'Miss Grainger,' he continued, 'I'm not aware of your personal circumstances so I don't know if this might potentially be good news or bad news, but have you considered the possibility that you might be pregnant?'

Somehow she'd managed the short journey back to her apartment. It must have been on autopilot as there'd been no conscious thought processes involved. Her mind was way too concerned with matters far more momentous.

She was pregnant.

It couldn't have been possible and she'd wanted to argue with the doctor. But with the very first test, a specimen she'd given the nurse, the results had confirmed what the physician had surmised during his examination.

And now she was having a baby, a *child*. She placed one hand over her abdomen in wonderment. Below her hand somewhere there was a tiny baby growing. And in only another six months or so that baby would be hers to hold.

There was too much to come to terms with. It was all too sudden—all too hard to believe. After all, she'd been having periods—admittedly irregular and not at all like normal, but that was half what she'd expected. Her own doctor had warned it could take a while for her cycle to settle down after taking her off the pill. She groaned at her own recklessness. It should have clicked that he'd been referring to ovulation as well.

And she'd told Paolo she was safe!

With a cry of despair, she dropped her head into her hands.

Things couldn't get any worse.

She wasn't just pregnant.

She was having Paolo's child!

And he would be furious. His words came back to her with chilling clarity. 'The last thing we both need is a baby, especially since we're about to become divorced.'

But the last thing they'd needed had happened. The last thing they'd wanted had happened.

For on the very same night they'd severed the only bond they'd had, they'd created another that would tie them together for ever.

She tried to laugh out loud with the irony of it all, but the only sound she could make came out brittle and false and couldn't be sustained anyway—not when all she really wanted to do was to descend into tears.

It was a mess, a horrible mess and there was no way out. And if it weren't bad enough that she had to come to terms with her newly found discovery herself, the knowledge she'd have to tell Paolo certainly was.

And he had to be told. Despite the reaction she knew she'd get, he had to know he was going to be a father and that she, Helene, the woman he'd just divorced, was going to have his child.

She'd contact his law firm, get them to put her in touch, find a way to tell him.

Assuming everything was all right.

She fished the appointment card for tomorrow's obstetric ultrasound from her purse, mulling over the doctor's words. Discarding the 'routine' and 'to confirm dates', she instead focused on what he'd really only hinted at—that the scan would show if her blood loss was caused by any underlying problems that could endanger, or might already have endangered, the life of her baby.

It was only another day. There was no point getting in touch with Paolo before then. Not if there was any chance…

With a sudden burst of guilt she threw herself out of her chair. She needed to get busy—keep busy. She wouldn't think about the possibilities. It didn't matter that she'd only just found out that she was pregnant. It didn't matter that she'd have to tell Paolo and that it would be the most difficult thing she had ever done. She would find a way to do that somehow.

What was paramount now was that her baby was healthy. She wouldn't think about the other options. She wouldn't wish this baby away. She couldn't do that to her child. Maybe she was new at this pregnancy business, but even she realised that this baby needed her to protect it and keep it safe. Even she knew that her baby needed her love. She wouldn't abandon it, as her parents had done to her, coldly cutting her off as if she'd never been their own. This baby would be wanted. It would be loved.

Work had granted her request to take the next day off, for which she was grateful. The scan was going to be hard enough to deal with without having to front her colleagues afterwards and pretend it was business as usual. She still had to get used to the idea she was pregnant herself.

From her windows overlooking Central Park, she could see it was a fine day, the gentle movement through the treetops signalling just a slight late-spring breeze. She slipped on a lightweight jacket over her linen dress and, doing her best to ignore the discomfort of holding onto the best part of a litre of water inside her, pulled open the door.

'Paolo!'

'We have to stop meeting like this,' he said, one side of his mouth angled up, although his cold eyes beamed imperiously down at her.

'What are you doing here? How did you find me?'

His eyebrows jagged upwards. 'And how lovely to see you too. Aren't you going to invite me in?'

'How did you get past Security?'

'Why aren't you at work?' he countered, ignoring

her questions and not waiting for an invitation as he pushed past her into the apartment. 'They told me you were taking sick leave.' His eyes narrowed as they raked over her, frankly assessing, taking in her coat and bag. 'But you don't look sick. And you're going out somewhere. So why would you be skipping work on such a beautiful day? Unless you're on your way to meet someone. Is that where you're going? You have a man waiting for you?'

She stayed where she was at the door, the shock at his sudden appearance turning into a slow-simmering resentment. 'I don't remember inviting you in.'

His gaze moved from her to scan the apartment and its contents. She got the distinct impression he was taking inventory. Then his eyes zapped back onto hers.

'Is there a man? Is that why you're going out?'

'Paolo, just stop it. This is crazy. What are you doing here? Did I miss a signature somewhere?'

His eyes blazed cold heat down upon her. 'Oh, no, you signed every last place. You didn't miss one.'

Confusion jangled with her thoughts. If she hadn't blown his chances for a speedy divorce, then why was he turning up now looking so upset? If he'd got what he wanted, why did his words sound so damning?

'So why are you here?'

'Why didn't you tell me you were coming to New York?'

Anger surged through her veins, escalating with every pump of her heart.

'You didn't ask.'

'You left, without a word—'

'I left a note!'

'That said nothing!'

'What did you expect me to say? *Happy divorce?*' She took a deep breath and put a hand to her forehead, though the discomfort she was experiencing was coming from a much lower region of her body. If she didn't calm down it wouldn't only be her blood pressure that burst. 'What's going on, Paolo?'

He took a step closer, his eyes hooded and dark, his expression grim.

'I came to see you as it happens. I found out where you were working and decided to look you up—*for old times' sake.*' He just about spat the words out. 'I didn't realise you'd be otherwise engaged.'

She glanced at her watch, anxious to be away.

'Late for your assignation?' he accused.

'Late for my appointment. I have to go.'

'And you expect me to let you.'

'As it happens, no. I have a much better idea.' She caught the look of surprise on his face and knew it was almost worth the change in plans to pull the rug out from underneath his arrogant feet. 'I think it's far better that you accompany me.'

Immediately his brow furrowed, calculating. 'Why? Where are you going?'

'You mean you don't know? And yet you seemed so certain a minute ago. Not that it's any business of yours, but I do expect to meet a man, actually. I think you should come along and meet him too. Just don't get upset if he makes me take my clothes off.'

He covered the distance between then them in an instant, gripping onto her shoulders, so tight that she knew instinctively that if her legs gave way she still wouldn't drop an inch.

'What are you talking about? Tell me.'

The power came off him in waves, the pure animal aggression that no doubt cut swathes through boardroom bureaucracy and decimated his courtroom opposition. His eyes glowered darkly down on her, his nostrils flaring, his signature male scent tugging at her senses.

It could tug all it liked. She'd been intoxicated by the man that night in Paris, but she wasn't about to make the same mistake now. Not now when she was so damned angry.

She looked squarely into his eyes and met them head-on. 'I'm having a scan. An obstetric ultrasound.'

'What for? What's going on?'

But even as he fired at her the questions it was clear that the cogs of his mind were spinning fiercely, searching for answers, clicking into place. She watched his face change, move through the stages of confusion, uncertainty, disbelief.

'But that would mean...'

And the swirling unknowns cleared from his dark eyes as she witnessed the moment, the very instant that realisation crystallised in his mind, and he knew.

She nodded. 'Congratulations. ''That would mean'' exactly that.'

He wheeled away, his hands releasing her from their iron grip so suddenly she had to fight at first to find her balance.

'So you're pregnant!'

Her confidence evaporated as she stared at his back, at the broad sweep of his shoulders now turned away from her. She couldn't blame him for the accusatory tone or for his reaction. After all, she'd been the one to claim she was safe. 'Apparently so. The scan is to check that everything is progressing okay.' He didn't move and painful protests from her swollen bladder spurred her into action. 'Look, I know it's a bit much to absorb, but I really should get to my appointment.'

She was pregnant. *Dio.* What timing! He'd tried to ignore the dreams that had dogged him ever since that night in Paris. He'd thought he'd forget, he'd thought his memories would fade and die in the harsh light of her cold departure. But something had happened that night to him and the memories wouldn't fade. Instead they had taunted him, becoming more vivid, more demanding as the weeks had gone by.

And finally a chance comment from a colleague, no more than a mere mention during a case that the International Bureau of Women's headquarters was right here in New York, and instinctively he'd known that this must have been where she'd come. All this time she'd been living in the same city and he'd had no idea.

Then the thought of being so close to her had driven his dreams to new heights, his needs to new levels. So why fight it? Why couldn't they see each other again? There was no rule that said they shouldn't.

And now, when he'd finally managed to track her down, it was all too late!

It was bad enough when he'd merely thought she was just planning on meeting someone. The possessive urge he'd had to physically restrain her from going had taken him by surprise. Her taunt about taking off her clothes had set his brain searing to white-hot mode. But then why wouldn't it? In all the weeks since he'd seen her, not once had he imagined her in someone else's arms—*in someone else's bed*—and the knowledge that she could turn over her lovers so quickly had hit him like a blow to the gut.

But it was worse than that.

She was pregnant. Having someone else's baby. And he could see her now with that child, maybe a little girl tugging on her mother's skirt, with soft wavy hair and green eyes just like her mother's...

The concept left him with a very bad taste in his mouth. Helene sure hadn't been wasting her time in New York as he had, that was a certainty.

'Paolo? I'm late for my appointment.'

He spun around, exhaling a breath that said it all as he strode past her into the lobby. He had something that he'd left off doing and there was no time like the present.

'Then don't let me keep you. I'll see myself out.'

He bypassed the lifts and strode straight for the fire escape. He wasn't in the mood to wait for anything.

'Paolo?'

The round English way she said his name carried softly down the hall. He stopped, his hand poised over the stairwell door handle. He looked over his shoulder to see her still framed in the doorway, much as she'd been when she'd first opened it, except her features now appeared more bewildered than shocked.

'Yes?' he asked her.

'You're not coming with me?'

Come with her? She had to be kidding. Hadn't that just been part of her game?

'Why should I?' he said, looking to turn the words

that had seared so deep back onto her. 'Just so I can see you take your clothes off for another man?'

Her spine must have stiffened then, to add so many apparent inches to her height, because her whole bearing suddenly seemed different—more aggressive, more challenging—her eyes cold and frosty.

'Up to you. I don't really care,' she said in a tone that made it abundantly clear that she did. 'I just thought that, seeing as you were here, you'd want to come along.'

He felt his eyes narrow even as his grip tightened on the fire-escape door handle. He should walk out now, leave Helene and her mess and any fantasies he'd had of looking up a woman he'd had trouble forgetting. But something else was happening here, something unsettling and disturbing that turned the air to crackling between them. He couldn't leave, not yet.

'Give me one good reason why,' he said when he could stand the frigid silence no longer.

She looked at him for a few seconds more without answering, her green eyes almost too large in her otherwise perfect face.

'Because it's your baby, Paolo. You're my baby's father.'

CHAPTER FOUR

THE lift doors pinged open between them, an incongruously cheerful sound in the otherwise tinder-dry atmosphere. A couple, a mother and daughter carrying numerous shopping bags, spilled out, their bright chatter halting as they stepped into the hallway and took in the scene—the woman standing rigid at the door; the man, his expression grim, poised to leave via the stairs—before they both bolted for the sanctuary of their apartment.

A second later Paolo crossed to Helene's door and bundled her inside.

'What do you mean?' he demanded, his tone brusque, his manner aggressive.

She pushed away his hands from her arms, her eyes blazing. 'What is there not to understand? I'm having your baby.'

'You're lying!'

'Excuse me? I think I'd be in a better position to know who the father is than you are.'

'How can you be sure it's mine?'

'We had sex, Paolo. I believe that's usually a reasonable indication where conception results.'

'That doesn't answer my question. How do I know I'm the only one?'

She sucked in a furious breath. 'What are you implying—that I sleep around? What kind of woman do you think I am?'

'Based on my limited experience of you—what do you expect me to think?'

Fury mounted within her. 'It's *your* child, Paolo,' she heaved through gritted teeth. 'You'd better get used to the idea, because it's the truth.'

'And it never occurred to you to let me in on "the truth" until I just happened to drop by? How convenient was that? What's the problem? Are you so desperate to pin this baby on someone you took the first guy who walked through the door?'

'No! It's not like that. This is your baby. Yours!'

'So when were you going to tell me? We spent the night together nearly three months ago. When were you going to let me in on the big secret? Or were you hoping to keep it a secret? To shut me out!'

'Why would I do that?'

'Because you couldn't wait to get away from me that night in Paris. You slunk off without a word, without an address or contact number. You never wanted to see me again and this baby, if it is mine, would make no difference to you.'

She shook her head. 'No. I only just found out myself. I had no idea until yesterday. And I was going to tell you anyway, but not until after the scan.'

'You expect me to believe that?'

'It's the truth,' she said flatly. 'Take it or leave it.'

He strode to the windows, his hand raking through his hair.

'I don't understand how this could have happened,' he said. 'You told me you were protected.'

'I know.' Her voice faltered. 'I thought I was safe.'

'You *thought* you were!'

'Hey, you didn't even bother to ask until after we'd

made love the first time. And I didn't see you breaking out the condoms!'

'Because you said you were safe!'

'I'm sorry. I made a mistake.'

'That's one hell of a mistake!'

'You're dead right. And I'm beginning to think it was neither my first nor my biggest mistake that night.'

She hitched her bag higher up her shoulder. 'I have to go now. So if you'll excuse me.'

She went to move past him, but his hand seized upon her forearm, locking her to the spot.

'Not so fast.' His eyes bored into hers, as hard and unforgiving as granite, 'If this is my baby—'

'It *is* your baby! There is no doubt of that. I can only pray it doesn't take after you.'

He blinked at her comment, slow and hard, the lines of his face rigid. 'Then I'm coming with you.'

'You know,' she said, 'I thought I was doing the right thing, but I really wish I hadn't told you. I wish I'd let you walk down those stairs and out of my life like you wanted to when you thought I must have been fooling around with someone else. Because right now I don't want to have a thing to do with you. And I certainly don't want you coming with me.'

'Too late,' he said, marching her towards the lifts. 'If you want to turn my life upside down with news like this, then you can expect me to hang around and deal with it.'

He was still holding onto her when they reached the lobby. The doorman snapped to attention as soon as they appeared. 'Winston,' Paolo ordered before she'd had a chance to open her mouth, 'we need a taxi. Ms Grainger has the address.'

'Yessir, Mr Mancini. A pleasure to help you.'

She didn't have time to ask him what was going on. Within a few seconds Winston had a taxi pulling into the kerb. 'A real pleasure, Mr Mancini, Ms Grainger. You look after that grandson of mine—he's going to make a fine lawyer one day.'

'I know,' Paolo said, slipping the man a tip, no doubt not the first for the day. 'He's one of our most promising recruits.'

Once in the cab he finally released his grip on her arm. She rubbed the place where his hand had branded her.

'I wondered how you'd made it past Security.'

He gave a nonchalant flick of his head, fixing his gaze out of the window on the passing traffic. 'I would have found a way.'

Somehow she didn't doubt it. It was the second time he'd bypassed Security to get directly to her door. What would it take if she really wanted to keep him out of her life?

Paolo remained sullen and silent the entire journey while she sat alongside him, her teeth troubling her bottom lip. Her biggest problem an hour ago had been making it to the clinic with her bladder intact. That short-term concern faded to insignificance, though, against her worries as to how Paolo would react. What would he expect? What would he demand? It was difficult enough coming to terms with the idea she was going to have a child without the added complication of not knowing how he stood on the issue. He wanted family, she knew that much. But that hardly meant he wanted an illegitimate child with the woman he'd just divorced.

'You don't need to come in with me,' she said, clambering awkwardly out of the cab when they'd pulled up outside the clinic. 'Why don't you wait for me out here?'

'No way,' he snapped, alighting and taking hold of her arm again. 'I'm coming with you.'

She tilted her chin, looking up at him, the sun behind his head turning his features dark and unreadable although she could tell he was furious. 'I'll let you know the results,' she insisted.

'I want to hear it firsthand. I have a couple of questions I wouldn't mind asking myself.'

Inwardly she groaned, having no doubt that his first question would be aimed squarely at establishing whether he could be the father. Why the hell had she asked him to come? She didn't want the first glimpse of her baby to be marred by the presence of someone determined to turn the proceedings into a battleground, father or no.

He tugged on her arm, ushering her towards the main entrance, and something inside her snapped. She wrenched her arm from his grip.

'You don't have to manhandle me. I can make it inside on my own. I'm not planning on making a break for it.'

His sun-drenched presence blasted pure heat back at her, but he said nothing, just turned and took the steps two at a time. She followed more slowly, using the handrail to help haul herself up. Not too much longer, she told herself resolutely, and she could rid herself of this pressing urge.

She reached the doors only to find Paolo standing in front waiting for her. *If only he were going to be as easy to dispense with.*

'What's wrong?' he asked her, for the first time a hint of concern edging his words. 'You look like you're in pain.'

'I *am* in pain!'

'Why? What's wrong?' he said. 'Do you need a doctor?'

She pulled herself up straight, wishing he would get out of the way so she could just get inside. 'After holding onto a litre of water for the last hour it's not exactly a doctor I need right now.' She pushed past him, trying unsuccessfully not to breathe in the spice of his cologne, the masculine essence of him. 'If you'll excuse me.'

He wouldn't let her check in. Instead he started barking orders for her immediate attention that had her cringing. He got results, though, as receptionists and orderlies rushed to meet his demands. The wheel-chair, though, was the final straw.

'I don't need a wheelchair!' she said to anyone who would listen. Nobody did. They were all too busy taking orders from Paolo.

She was whisked away to a cubicle and allowed to change into a robe in peace before the radiographer collected her. Paolo tried to follow.

'I'm afraid not,' the radiographer said, barring his way into the examination room. 'I'll let you in once I know everything is all right.'

'What do you mean?' he demanded. 'Why shouldn't it be all right?'

'It's routine. It's nothing to worry about.'

'But what could be wrong?'

Helene took in a calming breath. 'I've had some bleeding. The doctor doesn't think it's a problem, but they just need to confirm the pregnancy is progressing normally first.'

'That's right,' the radiographer agreed, 'and as soon as we know that, then I'll invite you to come and see the images. So if you'll excuse us?'

Paolo wheeled away, his features clearly showing his resentment at being shut out of what he considered something he had more of a stake in than a man merely operating a machine.

'First baby?' the radiographer inquired, making idle chatter as he got her settled on the bed and ready for the scan. 'Dad seems to be a bit strung out.'

Strung out probably didn't come close to how Paolo was feeling right now. She'd had a day to come to terms with her new state and it was still a struggle. Paolo hadn't had an hour.

'He's got a lot on his mind,' she replied noncommittally.

Ten minutes later the radiographer opened the door. Paolo burst into the room like a rodeo bull on steroids, powerful and angry and ready to take on all comers. It didn't take much to imagine steam coming from his flaring nostrils.

'What news?'

The radiographer recoiled, resuming his seat and angling the screen towards them.

'See for yourself.' He placed the sensor back on her abdomen and slid it over the skin.

Paolo knew he was supposed to be watching the screen, but somehow the thought of someone else touching Helene's bare flesh, even if indirectly, set his blood to boiling point and it was impossible to drag his eyes away.

There was something on her skin, something slippery that allowed the instrument to slide across the surface and gave her creamy flesh a satiny gloss. His gut clenched as he remembered. He'd felt that skin, pressed up against his own, he'd tasted every square inch of her and had thought about tasting more every night since then.

As he wanted her now. Even though she was pregnant, possibly with his own child, one snatch of skin and he wanted her more than ever.

'There's your baby.'

The radiographer's words sliced through his thoughts and desires and finally he turned his attention to the image on the screen. He felt his gaze focus more intently. It was amazing, just so incredibly clear, lying with legs crossed, a hand clearly resting by its cheek. And possibly…

'It's incredible,' Helene said.

'How many weeks along is it?' he demanded, holding his breath.

'Well,' the radiographer said, oblivious to the atmosphere in the room while busy manipulating the monitor to get an even sharper image, 'the measurements I took will be more accurate, but I'd hazard a guess that this little one is about twelve weeks along. Does that sound about right to you?'

'That's right.' He saw Helene mouth the words, but he heard nothing but the tidal wave of blood that crashed through his senses.

It was his child. It had to be. The tiny creature with

the transparent legs, the tiny fingers and toes and the huge shadowy eyes was his baby!

'What's that?' he asked, pointing to a flickering shape on the screen.

The radiographer checked where Paolo was indicating. 'Ah, that's your baby's heart.'

'*Dio,*' he said, in awe and wonderment. His child's heart. Beating and pulsing with life already. It was almost too much to comprehend.

Someone was talking, but it was too unimportant compared to the new life he was witnessing on the screen.

'Mr Grainger, would you like to take a photograph of the baby home?'

'Oh, no,' Helene said. 'We're not mar—'

'What *my wife* means,' Paolo said, cutting her off mid-stream, and patting her on the hands affectionately, 'is that she kept her maiden name when we married. My name is Mancini. Isn't that right, darling?'

'What did you mean back there?' Helene asked once they were back at her apartment. 'Why the pretence that we were man and wife?'

'It's no pretence,' he said. 'We've been married for years.'

'But the divorce? I signed those papers months ago. It should be through by now.'

'It would have been.' He shrugged.

'What do you mean?' she insisted. 'What are you saying? You *did* lodge those papers, didn't you?'

The silence stretched out between them and yet Paolo made no attempt to ease the mounting tension.

She shook her head, scarcely able to believe the truth his reticence had confirmed.

'You didn't lodge them. Why on earth not?'

His eyes surveyed her coldly and she wondered why. It wasn't as if the divorce had been her idea. She hadn't been the one pounding on his door in the middle of the night to wind up their marriage.

'I didn't have time. I had to come back to the States and finish off a case.'

'So, that means—technically—we're still married?'

'Technically, yes.'

She crossed to the window, gazing out over the treetops to the buildings beyond.

Still married. And yet he'd seemed in such a desperate rush to be done with her.

She licked her lips. 'So when are you planning on lodging the papers?'

People were rushing along the pavement below, either swinging briefcases or shopping bags or jumping in and out of the never-ending sea of yellow taxis. People were in a hurry to go somewhere.

Yet inside her temporary home the world seemed to have slowed down as time strung out between them. She knew when he moved in close behind her, but she sensed his presence rather than heard his hushed footfall on the carpeted floor.

She found his reflection in the glass, saw his hands hesitate on their way to her shoulders and fall away again.

'What are your plans?' he asked.

She spun around, taken aback by the question. 'What do you mean?'

'Are you giving up your job?'

'Why would I do that? I love my job.'

'You are planning on having this baby?' His words were framed as a question, but his tone carried a thinly veiled message. There was only one answer as far as Paolo was concerned. Well, so be it, but why did he have to be so convinced that she would not do the right thing by her child?

'First you believe me capable of flitting from bed to bed with any number of men upon whom I can pin my baby, and then you seem to think I could destroy the incredible brand new life that we both witnessed today.

'You saw it, Paolo, I know you did. This baby isn't some vague concept, it's a life, with a heart and brain and fingers and toes. How could you even think I could try to undo what we've created, even if by accident?' She took a deep breath, letting it out slowly. 'You obviously have a very low opinion of me.'

He brushed her protest aside with the wave of one hand. 'But for all that you still intend to work.'

'For as long as I can, yes.'

'What about the baby?'

She moved to the other side of the room before turning to face him. She needed to put distance between them to dilute his impact. 'I'm pregnant, Paolo. I'm not ill. There's no reason I can't work till I'm seven or eight months pregnant. Lots of women do.'

'Not when they're having my child, they don't!'

'Oh? And exactly how many women are we talking about?'

As soon as she'd let the words go she realised how stupid they sounded. He hadn't had a chance to have children because he'd never had a chance to commit to anyone—not while he'd been married to her and protecting her from Khaled. She dropped her face in her hands and breathed deep before waving away her comment with one hand.

'I didn't mean that, Paolo. I'm sorry. But, honestly, I'll be fine.'

'What about the problems you mentioned—the bleeding?'

'It shouldn't be a problem. Today's scan showed everything was normal. You saw the doctor's report—he thinks it was probably just due to hormonal fluctuations. So there's no reason for me to stop working just yet.'

'And what about when the baby comes? Then what will you do in your apartment all by yourself?'

She turned away, searching for answers in the plate-glass windows. 'I… I don't know—take leave—I haven't had time to think about it. I'll work something out, though.'

'Then don't bother,' he said emphatically. 'I have already come up with a solution.'

Cold tentacles of dread clutched at her insides and squeezed tight. He sounded much too sure—much too confident for her liking—and she felt her handle on the situation slipping away.

'I'm certainly willing to hear your input,' she maintained shakily. 'This baby belongs to both of us. There's no reason why we can't work something out together.'

'There's no need. I have the only practical solution.'

'What do you mean?'

'You will come and live with me in my villa in

Milan. I have almost concluded this case; it's time I was returning home. And you will have everything you need. I will look after you and the baby.'

'But, Paolo, that's not practical. I live in Paris. And our divorce will be through ten minutes after you lodge those papers.'

'Then I simply won't lodge them,' he said.

'Why?' she asked. 'What do you mean?'

He moved closer until he was standing directly in front of her, his mouth tilted in victory, his dark chocolate eyes so satisfied they should have been tinged with cream. Then he reached up one hand to grace her cheek.

'It's quite simple,' he said, so close that his breath fanned softly against her face. 'As far as the law is concerned, we're married. And,' he said, after giving her just a moment to assimilate that fact, 'for the time being, we're going to stay married.'

CHAPTER FIVE

'I DON'T understand,' Helene said, shaking her head against the palm of Paolo's hand, trying to suppress the flare of hope that sparked into life inside her, battling to make sense of his unexpected announcement. 'You initiated this divorce. Now you're saying you've changed your mind?'

'Now we have someone else to consider. I don't want my child to be considered illegitimate. We should stay married, at least until the baby is born.'

It took only a second for it to sink in. His sudden interest in staying married had nothing to do with her. He was protecting the child. It wasn't that he wanted to divorce her any less. It wasn't his intention that had changed, merely the timing.

She clamped down on a dank bubble of disappointment. For while logic told her that of course that was what he'd meant, irrationally part of her wished he'd been having second thoughts for an entirely different reason, such as whatever had brought him to her door today in the first place.

'What are you thinking?'

His question snapped her attention back to him. 'I'm thinking you're expecting a lot to ask me to give up my life in Paris to come and stay with you, just because I'm pregnant.'

One eyebrow arched high as his head tilted. 'And

it wasn't asking me a lot to marry you twelve years ago to save you from Khaled?'

'Don't hit me with the guilt thing. It's hardly the same thing. You continued with your life. I didn't expect you to live with me.'

'It's very much the same thing. I did something for you—for twelve years. Don't you think there were things I gave up, that I might have done, if not for my marriage to you?'

Oh, God, she thought, jamming her eyes shut. Of course he had. He'd given up the chance to marry Sapphire, the woman he loved, before she was stolen away from him.

She'd cost him his lover and his future and yet now she was acting as if she were the victim. And it wasn't as if he'd asked for this baby. They'd both known the risks and she'd guaranteed him there was none. She could hardly take the higher moral ground.

'I'm sorry,' she said, knowing her words were painfully inadequate, 'I didn't mean—'

'So now you do something for me. And for our child.' His eyes glinted dangerously. 'And in six months, when our child has been delivered, you can still have your divorce.'

The word hissed through his teeth like a curse and she shuddered.

'And if I don't want to give up my job?' she said, trying to infuse a degree of confidence into her voice. 'If I don't want to come to Milan?'

'Then I'll sue for sole custody and you'll lose the child altogether.'

She didn't doubt it. Even as the cold fingers of his control crawled down her spine she knew it was true.

With the resources of his legal practice and his family's wealth behind him, she wouldn't stand a chance, even as the child's biological mother. But could he be that ruthless?

'You wouldn't deprive me of my child!'

He held up one hand to silence her. 'It needn't come to that. All we have to do is to give the impression that we are a family. Surely you can do that until the baby arrives?'

A family. The word seemed almost foreign to her now. Long ago she'd thought she'd been part of a family, but those ideas had been shot to pieces when her father's wishes for her marriage to Khaled had been stymied. Then she'd realised she wasn't part of a family at all, rather she was part of their assets, her life played out as if in a shop window, ready to be sold off to the customer who paid the highest price. And since then she'd been alone for such a long time.

Yet the concept of family tugged at her senses in a way that drew her inexorably to his proposal.

'You want us to act like a real family—why?'

'My mother is getting older. She wants to see me married and settled down. She wants more grandchildren. I can now give her one but her joy will be nothing compared to that she would get if she thought I was married.'

'And—after the baby is born?'

Her heart hammered loud in her chest. This was her moment of truth. Surely he would not insist she leave her newborn child and return to Paris. Surely he could not expect any mother to do such a thing.

'*Sì*,' he acknowledged with a nod, 'she would be disappointed that the marriage did not last. But by then she would have her grandchild to dote upon. The pain would soon pass.'

Her breath caught in her throat. *What of her pain?* Her life seemed to be turning into a series of rejections from Paolo. How much more could she bear? The wedding night and his desperate late-night rush to have her complete the divorce papers—if those occasions hadn't been rejection enough, now he was planning to dispense with her again just as soon as her baby was delivered.

'And when would I be able to see my child?'

'We would arrange visiting rights, as do other divorced couples.'

'But you would expect custody.'

He shrugged. 'Of course. Besides, a child will only stifle your career. I know you care too much for that to happen.'

'You make it sound like I would neglect my own child and yet your career is not something you can toss aside either.'

'But you are alone. Who would look after the baby when you are at work?'

'There are childcare places—nannies—'

'I will not have my child taken care of by strangers! In Milan the child will have family, my mother, its cousins, when I am not able to be there. Can you not see that this will be better for the child?'

'You don't seem to give me much choice.'

'You have no choice. This is the best possible arrangement.'

'No! It might be for you, but not for me or the child.'

'For all of us! Look at it this way,' he said. 'For

twelve years I put up with a marriage of convenience. All I'm asking of you is a fraction of that. Six months in a family of convenience. Six months compared to twelve years—surely that's not too much to ask?'

It was way too much to ask. The closer it came to their departure day, the more convinced of that she was. He'd organised her flights, her removal from her apartment and already he'd teed up appointments with specialists for her the moment they arrived back in Milan. He'd left her nothing to do but to sort out her personal effects here in her apartment prior to packing.

Her arms full of books she'd collected during her stay, she paused on her way to the packing box and gazed out over the park.

He'd done everything, even overseeing her application to take extended leave without pay from her work. He was taking no chances that she'd change her mind about not working once she returned to Europe.

He'd taken over her life.

In two days they would leave for Milan where she would be expected to live in the Mancini villa for the next six months, pretending to be Paolo's whirlwind wife. His *real* wife, not just his wife on paper.

She wasn't sure if she could do it. She wasn't even sure if she liked him any more. Gone was the man who'd turned up at her apartment that night, leaving in place an angry stranger who held her responsible for everything that had gone wrong in his life, from the loss of Sapphire to her unplanned pregnancy.

Well, maybe she was and maybe living in close proximity to Paolo for six months was her penance.

No, penance was way too easy, she decided, dropping the books into the box. Hers was a life sentence.

She moved into the bedroom and was putting away some earrings from her dresser when she found it. In the bottom corner of her small *cloisonné* jewellery box she'd had since a child was the ring Paolo had given her on their wedding day. Paolo's signet ring.

She slipped it on and watched as its square ebony face immediately fell to the back of her finger. She smiled. It was way too big for her. It always had been. They'd both stressed so much about escaping from her family and getting married as soon as they could that they'd completely forgotten they needed a ring.

When the registrar had asked for it during the brief ceremony there'd been a hushed silence, stunned looks and a scramble to find something, anything, that would do the job. Paolo had finally wrenched off his signet ring and placed the warm metal on her finger, holding her fingers together so that it couldn't slip around.

She held her hand up now, feeling the weight of the chunky ring on her fingers. After the wedding she'd tried to give it back, but he'd told her it was hers and she'd treasured it, wearing it on her thumb and holding it close to her heart at night. Only later, after one scare where she'd thought she'd lost it that had had her searching her room for days, she'd relegated it to the safety of her jewellery box.

Sighing, she slipped the ring off and placed it back in the box. It was a memento of a different time, a time long gone, when Paolo had been her knight in shining armour, saving her from a forced marriage to a man for whom she could feel nothing but hate.

But now Paolo was calling in the debt. No longer her saviour. This time he was her nemesis, forcing her into yet another arranged marriage.

A key turned in her lock and she gritted her teeth. Winston had organised a key for Paolo without blinking, obviously assuming she wouldn't object. But then, why wouldn't he think that? As far as she could see, nobody, but nobody, said no to Paolo Mancini.

Then he was standing in the doorway, larger than life, his height and his shoulders blocking out the light pouring through the windows behind him.

'I wish you wouldn't do that,' she said, assigning the small jewellery box to the pile designated for her carry-on luggage.

'Do what?'

'Let yourself in. You could knock.'

'What if something was wrong with you? What if you couldn't answer the door? You might be grateful for my attention then.'

'*Nothing* is going to happen. Don't you understand?'

'You're pregnant. You don't know that.'

'Listen, Paolo. Millions of women all over the world have babies every year without any worries at all.'

'And some don't. I don't see the point in taking any chances.'

She sighed, long and hard. There was no point arguing with him. He'd made up his mind that she was the least qualified to look after her own pregnancy. She was hardly going to convince him otherwise.

He strode to her wardrobe, checking the contents. 'You have much to do still.'

'It won't take long.'

'No, I'll get someone.'

Before she could protest he'd whipped out his cellphone and barked some orders as all the while her anger grew.

'You don't have to run my life, you know.'

'You're too slow. Besides, I want you to come with me. We have some business to attend to. This can all be handled while we're gone.'

'What business?'

'You'll see. Get your coat. I don't want you catching a chill.'

She brushed his order aside as she headed for the door, scooping up her bag on the way. She'd been out earlier, and in a mid-sleeved top and low-cut trousers she'd been more than adequately dressed for the day. 'I won't need it,' she said. 'It's a beautiful day—'

'Get your coat!'

She pursed her lips, forcing them to remain closed when all she wanted to do was to yell at him to get out of her life and leave her alone.

How could she ever have imagined she loved him? How could she have harboured secret hopes and dreams about him ever since that night in Paris? Not even the prospect of them having created a new life warmed him. He'd sucked out every last shred of joy she should have been feeling about having this child, just as he was sucking her life dry.

'Where are we going?' she asked at last when Winston had seen them into a cab.

'It's not far,' he said.

They turned left along Fifty-Ninth Street, past the drink vans and stalls lining the southern wall of Central Park and then into Fifth Avenue before coming to a stop.

'We're here?' she said. 'We could have walked.'

'I don't want you taking any unnecessary risks,' he said, ushering her out after paying the driver.

'Walking a kilometre or so hardly constitutes a risk.'

But he wasn't listening. Already he was shepherding her towards the imposing sandstone building. The flags caught her eye, flapping in the breeze over her head either side of the door. Then the name struck her. *Tiffany & Co.*

'What are we doing here?' she asked.

'You need something to look married. My mother will expect it.'

Look married? Fat chance. Hadn't it occurred to him that no ring in the world was going to convince anybody? That it would take more than just a gold band on her finger to give the impression they were a loving couple?

'I don't get this,' she said as, with one arm around her shoulders and the other holding her hand, he propelled her into the building. 'Do you really think that a lump of gold is going to magically transform us into the perfect couple?'

He snorted his disapproval as he steered her through the ground-floor shoppers.

Maybe that was what he wanted, though. Maybe

he wanted them to look unhappy. The long-suffering husband, the petulant wife. She could almost hear him bewailing his misfortune already—no wonder the marriage had come to a sticky end!

They must have been expected. After a word they were whisked away into a tasteful private consultation room and it seemed the riches of the world were on display before them.

'What style of engagement ring were you after, Ms Grainger?' the consultant asked when they were settled.

'Oh,' she said, taken aback that she was allowed to even have any say in the issue. Given Paolo's attitude of late, it was amazing he hadn't just had something delivered.

But she certainly didn't need an engagement ring. They'd never been engaged. Why add unnecessary expense to the deception? 'Just a wedding band will be fine.' After all, they had been married. Were married still.

Without moving his face the consultant flicked his eyes to Paolo.

'My fiancée is too unassuming,' he said. 'Of course she must have an engagement ring.' He looked down at the display, pointing one out to her. 'What about something like this?'

She suppressed a gasp when she saw where he was indicating. It was simply beautiful. One large diamond flanked by two almost as large that would make stunning solitaires by themselves. Together in their white gold setting they were just dazzling with brilliance. No doubt the dollars would be equally dazzling.

'I don't think so,' she said. 'Maybe something more simple.'

'Try it on,' he insisted, and the consultant immediately complied by removing the ring from the display and sliding it on her finger before she could object.

It was stunning, sparking light with every move of her hand. But a ring like that should be worn by a woman in love, given to her by the man in love with her. It didn't belong on the hand of a woman like her, a woman expected to live a lie for the next six months.

'I don't think so,' she said, with a tinge of regret as she took one final look. 'What else—'

'No,' Paolo said. 'We'll take that one. And a band to go with it.'

'You can't!' she protested.

'It's decided,' he said, brushing away her protests.

The consultant was away processing the transaction before a thought occurred to her.

'You're not getting a ring for yourself?'

He stood up.

'It's hardly necessary,' he said dismissively before striding his way across the room.

Of course it wasn't necessary. It was hardly necessary to weigh her down with what amounted to several carats either, but that hadn't stopped him. Yet he himself wouldn't stoop to wearing a ring that said they were in some way linked. Clearly he wanted nothing that reminded him of their marriage.

In a surge of frustration she headed for the opposite side of the room, barely registering the contents of the display cabinets despite their inherent beauty and style. Until a flash of colour caught her eye.

The rich red crystal was formed into a stylised heart shape, its softly rounded contours and lush Elsa Peretti design turning its colour anywhere from neon red to dark shadow as her eyes changed angles over it. It was so simple and yet so wonderfully evocative, probably one of the cheapest things in the store, but it was impossible to drag her eyes away.

Across the room Paolo knew he was better off staying right away from her. So long as he maintained his distance he had a chance of controlling the desire that burned inside, the need to possess her.

She was standing over the display case, totally absorbed in whatever was held there, and his eyes relished the opportunity to drink in her curves. He approved of the way the pregnancy was already making her look, her body subtly changing, her breasts heavier and rounder than they'd been. He wanted to peel her top from her right then and there and let them fall, plump and full, into his hands. He wanted to fill his mouth with their firm peaks.

He swallowed back a groan. The hunger for her was back, more than ever, the shock at finding out she was carrying his child a mere blip in his desire.

But he would wait. He would do nothing yet, not until the doctor gave the all-clear and he was sure he could not harm the baby. Then he would have six months with her in his villa, six months where she would be his, in body as well as in name.

He drew closer, telling himself he was only curious about whatever it was that had so captivated her, moving silently over the signature carpet. He breathed in a hint of her scent, the fresh smell of her hair, and he longed to wind it in his hands and pull her mouth to his once again. Instead he forced his gaze lower, down into the display case and whatever it was she was so taken by.

It was a paperweight, that was all, although there was something about it, something intriguing…

Then it hit him and he remembered—the scan, the transparent flesh, the easily recognisable bone structure from its corded spine to its minuscule toes, and the most amazing thing of all—the shadowed trace of a tiny heart beating.

His baby's heart.

'Il cuore del mio bambino,' he said, his breath stirring the feathered ends of her hair.

She jumped a little, turning her face over her shoulder, her lips parted, her eyes widening when she noticed how close he was. And for the first time he noticed the dark smudges under her eyes, the hint of strain stretching tight the muscles in her cheeks, and he felt his own brow pull into a frown. But before he could say anything the assistant signalled he was ready.

Without uttering a word, he peeled away from her, leaving her standing there while he concluded the transaction.

Helene struggled to catch her breath. He'd been so close. Too close. And he'd looked at her in a way she hadn't seen for days, his dark eyes steamed with desire. In a way that had brought back a night of passion in a Paris flat and the fires that had raged between them. Lately his eyes had been filled more with hostility and anger and an icy coldness that had frozen her spirit. The sudden thaw had taken her unawares.

What was he thinking about?

She huffed in a breath, hugging her sides and wishing he'd maintained his steely demeanour. If he was expecting her to walk out after six months, the last thing she wanted was a rekindling of the kind of fires that had already burned between them. For him it was obviously just physical. But for her it would be much more. The cost would be too great.

She wanted him to hate her. She needed to be able to hate him in return. Only then would she be able to walk out of this arrangement with her pride intact. It was going to be devastating enough as it was, given that she was expected to leave her baby behind. Her breath lurched as every muscle inside her clenched.

How the hell was she supposed to cope with that?

He couldn't make her do it. No one could expect her to just give birth and walk away, to relegate all maternal responsibilities to someone else. It wasn't right. It wasn't human.

She blinked as he shoved her coat towards her. Blankly she took it, turning toward the lifts. So he was finished. The deal was done. Signora Mancini would no doubt be suitably impressed by the glittering armoury of jewels he'd bestowed upon his 'wife'.

Similarly she'd be heart broken when said wife left, leaving a newborn baby in the care of its father.

And suddenly the reason for Paolo's easy extravagance hit home. Doubtless he'd insist she take the diamonds with her.

Her damnation in his family's eyes would be complete.

Such a generous husband.

Such a selfish and greedy wife.

Bile squeezed up in her throat as he ushered her to the lifts. She didn't want the rings. She couldn't wear them. She had one wedding ring already and it had been all she'd needed for all these years. Maybe it was worthless, compared to the dazzlers he'd bought today, but at least that one had been honestly given, in the spirit of the moment, something that had cost him a part of himself rather than meaningless dollars.

They reached the ground floor and she launched herself for the doorway to the outside as if it were a life-saver.

'Stop!' Out on the street he lunged for her arm, pulling her around. 'Stop!'

'No,' she said, pulling in the other direction, knowing the last thing she needed right now was to be cooped up in an enclosed space yet again with Paolo. What she needed was room to move, and air, and freedom. She yanked her arm free and crossed both in front of her. 'I need to walk.'

She headed in the direction of the park, not caring whether or not he followed. But of course he did. With a sharp intake of air, she reminded herself that his reaction was the only one she could have expected.

He was hardly about to let her go, not with his child on board.

Within a few metres he fell into a rhythm alongside her, matching her pace easily, his long legs making her naturally shorter steps look all the more hurried and desperate.

'Where do you think you're going?' he demanded.

'Anywhere you're not,' she snapped, without looking over at him, making an unheralded pitch towards Fifty-Ninth Street.

She knew she wouldn't get away. There was no hope of that. But just the momentary charge from having him following her, going where she wanted to go, after his stultifying presence the last few weeks—it was incredibly liberating.

'I'll get a cab.'

'You do that,' she said. 'I'm walking.'

She pushed her way through the ambling tourist traffic along the south-eastern boundary of Central Park, where the earthy smell of horses overtook the otherwise inescapable smells of the city. Brightly adorned carriages lined the road and lyrical Irish voices chatted amongst themselves or soothed their patient animals.

He looked more dominating than usual here, she thought, swinging her glance sideways, watching him striding purposefully along in his Armani suit amidst the camera-wielding tourists and street vendors. Totally out of place and yet still so supreme. But then it wouldn't matter where he was. The man was made to be noticed.

She drew closer to the head of the queue of carriages, feeling herself soothed with every step by the rhythmic clomp of hooves and the creak of wheels setting off with another load of sightseers for a tour around the park.

A sudden urge bit deep. She'd never once had the opportunity to give in to her desire for a circuit around the park and tomorrow they would leave.

A glimpse across to the man at her side told her

Paolo probably hadn't even registered there were horses here, his hooded gaze focused on the path directly ahead, his mind no doubt working on the next step in his plan to secure her child.

The driver of the lead carriage saw them coming. He stepped out to greet them, his satin vest glossy in the afternoon sun.

'Sir,' he said in his Emerald Isle brogue, 'would you like to take the beautiful lady for a spin around the park?'

But it was Helene who stopped and smiled.

'Thank you,' she said without hesitation. 'I believe he would.'

She allowed the driver to hand her up into the carriage and when she turned it was to see Paolo's brows drawn together, his expression quizzical as he gazed up at her. Pleasure zipped through her. It was exhilarating catching him unawares. He was so used to calling the shots.

'I thought you wanted exercise.'

'So I'm exercising my fun muscles. Climb aboard,' she invited. 'Yours could definitely do with a workout.'

A burst of laughter followed her challenge, but it didn't come from Paolo. 'I've a feelin' you might have met your match in your young lady,' the driver said with a wink.

She allowed herself a smile as Paolo said nothing, unbuttoning his jacket while sinking grim-faced into the plush upholstered seat alongside her, the driver meanwhile climbing up in front and collecting up the reins.

He flicked them twice. 'Gee up,' he said and the

powerful Clydesdale horse set off. The carriage lurched into action before settling into a smooth ride as they entered the park through the wide gates.

The city melted away behind them as they cruised along the shaded avenue, the towers and buildings soon replaced by massive trees and wall-to-wall greenery, the permanent traffic noises muted by the sound of birds, the splash of water and the lilting rendition of an Irish ballad. Red squirrels darted between the trees and the sunlight made crazy patterns through the foliage.

Despite Paolo's presence, she found herself relaxing for the first time since she'd discovered the pregnancy. She closed her eyes and leant back, breathing in deeply and enjoying the gentle rocking rhythm of the carriage. It was good to be outside. It was good to have a chance to think.

'We have some matters to discuss.' Paolo's rich tones permeated her consciousness, but she refused to let his words disturb her reverie.

'Go ahead,' she said, still not opening her eyes, 'if you must.'

'It would be more private in your apartment.'

She snapped her eyes open, saw him weighing up their proximity to the driver.

'Not if the minions you've organised to pack my gear are there, it won't be. The driver is singing; he can't hear you. So long as you don't shout at me, that is.'

For a second his eyes sparked displeasure and the muscles in his jaw clenched and she could see he'd like nothing more than to shout at her right now. But then he blinked and took a deep breath, eventually turning side on to face her and sliding one arm along the back of the seat.

'I telephoned my mother to let her know to expect us. I told her about the baby.'

'How did she take it?'

His head tilted. 'Naturally she's excited, although she would have preferred it if we'd been married before the baby came along.'

'I thought we *were* married.'

'There's no point telling anyone about that, let alone my mother. I said we were married on impulse a week ago in a register office here in New York.'

'So now she thinks that I was careless enough to get pregnant and you decided to marry me just to do the honourable thing?'

'Isn't that more or less how it is?'

'No!' She could see the case building up against her. The inconvenient circumstances of their quick marriage, the woman he'd done the right thing by marrying and taking for his own, the woman who would betray him and walk away from her child with a handful of diamonds.

'She wanted to have another ceremony, a blessing, performed in Milan, but I told her to wait until after the baby as you were worried about your figure.'

'Oh, lovely, thank you.' She leaned back against the seat, pressing her eyes shut as mentally she added vanity to the list of her transgressions. But what did she expect? There was no way that Paolo was going to admit to his mother that a blessing didn't suit him given his intention to dispose of his temporary wife the first chance he got.

'Is there anything else I should know?'

For a moment all she heard was the clop of the horse's hooves and the quiet croon of the driver.

'I told her that you were a very beautiful woman.'

Just vain, greedy and selfish. She took a deep breath. If his comment was supposed to be some sort of compliment it hardly made up for the faults he'd already attributed to her in abundance. 'I'm not sure I can go through with this,' she whispered, looking up into the treetops for solace, her earlier feelings of peace and serenity shattered.

'You will go through with this.' He took her chin in one hand, steering her face around to face his. 'Because you owe me. You know you do.'

She swallowed as dark eyes held her own and she knew that what he said was true. He'd put aside any hope of having a family for years while he'd honoured his promise to her. Now he was calling in the debt. Now he was exacting repayment. Okay, so she owed him, but did he have to take over her life as if he owned it? Did he have to take over their child as though it were his alone?

She looked into his eyes, searching for reason, praying for understanding. Couldn't he see that he was asking too much?

But his gaze failed to offer her answers; instead it seemed to be seeking answers of its own. The place where his hand touched her chin prickled with awareness as his fingers shifted subtly over her skin. The lashes framing his eyes suddenly seemed darker, his gaze a heated caress that whispered over her skin, and she knew instinctively by the way her body reacted that he was thinking about a night they'd shared in Paris those few months ago.

Then conflict and confusion muddied their dark depths and he broke his gaze away, dropping his hand and sweeping it back through his hair. Embarrassed, she turned away to look out of the carriage, feigning interest in the view and feeling strangely let down.

He coughed, low and rough, and she got the impression he was clearing his mind of the unwelcome images as much as clearing his throat.

'Apart from my mother,' he said after a few awkward moments, 'you will meet my younger sister, Maria, and her husband, Carlo. They have two small children.'

She looked back over at him. 'And your father?'

'He's dead.'

His flat response was clearly designed to be a full stop to the topic. She studied his face and the fierce set of his chin and thought about pressing him for more details. After all, they really knew so little about each other when they were supposed to be happy newly-weds—surely it would be normal to know more of his family history? But his eyes looked so pained and ill at ease that she desisted. It was obviously not a topic that he wanted her to pursue.

'I'm sorry,' she said.

His jaw clenched. 'It is my mother who I am concerned about right now. She is not happy about missing our so-called wedding.'

'That's hardly surprising,' she offered, happy to go with the change of topic. 'Who would want to miss their child's wedding?'

Other than her own parents, of course.

She looked down at the fingers tangled together in her lap and wished so much that things had worked out differently. As far as her parents were concerned she didn't exist any more. Had never existed. They would never know that she was a mother, that they had a grandchild.

A choking feeling grabbed her throat as tears pricked her eyes, threatening to unleash themselves and spill over. She blinked rapidly, struggling to keep them at bay.

Damn! She pulled a tissue from a pocket and pressed it to her nose, squeezing tightly. She hadn't thought about her parents for ages, much less made herself cry over them. This pregnancy was turning her emotions upside down. In the space of a few hours she'd gone from anger to light-heartedness and all stops in between and now she was plunging headlong into the depths of gloom.

'Are you going to tell your parents about the baby?'

She swung her head around. Did he know what she was thinking?

'I can't see the point. They haven't bothered to contact me in twelve years.'

'But it's their grandchild. Surely they have a right to know.'

She wanted to agree with him, but she couldn't bring herself to do it. 'Maybe. In a perfect world. But family obviously isn't as important as the bottom line where I come from. As far as my family is concerned, I cost them, so now I'm paying the consequences for my actions.'

'Your father was wrong to treat you like that, like some kind of asset only there to produce him a return. He was expecting too much.'

The irony wasn't lost on her.

'Oh, and you're not?' But this was about her parents. She shook her head and continued. 'Look, it doesn't matter. It amounts to the same thing. And if I told them about the baby and they didn't want to know, I'd hate myself for letting them know I cared enough to tell them and giving them the opportunity for rejecting me once again.'

'They should care,' he said solemnly.

'That may be true,' she agreed. 'Although, let's face it, even if they did and were happy about it, is there any chance they'd get to see their grandchild? It sounds to me like you've got the access situation all tied up.'

She noticed the spike of anger in his eyes and was surprised. She hadn't meant to go on the attack, but it was a fair point. There was little incentive she'd want her parents to know anyway, given their predilection for treating children as something that could be bartered or traded like a business asset, but that didn't mean she had to defend Paolo's actions.

As it was, he'd arranged everything to suit himself, without regard for her feelings or even for the child that would be forced to grow up separated from its mother.

'You resent me for wanting the best for this child,' he said.

'And don't you think I do?'

'You'll always be this baby's mother. No one is denying that.'

'But you expect to keep the child with you. You won't let me take it.'

'That's out of the question,' he hissed, his voice

tight and tense and inviting no argument. 'The baby will stay with me.'

The baby—but not her. He couldn't have said it any clearer painted in the sky in letters sixty feet high. The meaning would be the same. He expected her to go and he expected her to leave her child with him when she did.

She turned her face away, her knuckles aching from pressing her fingers into her palms. She wanted to cry. She wanted to scream. She wanted to jump up and down and make him see that what he was doing was simply wrong and that she wanted no part of it.

But that way wouldn't work with him. He was used to arguing with the best people in the legal fraternity. There was no way she would sway him with her simple words or raw emotion.

She would have to come up with some way that would make him see that she deserved one heck of a lot more than being put out to pasture once she'd delivered his child, something that would change his mind about making her leave.

The carriage pulled out of the shadowed park and onto the shoulder and she blinked with the sudden change of light.

'Helene,' he said, 'I want you to have this.'

He pulled a neat blue box tied with a white ribbon from his jacket pocket. She shook her head and pulled away. The rings could wait. She could put them on the minute before they arrived at the villa for all the good they would do her. 'Maybe later,' she said, looking away again.

'No,' he urged. 'Take it.'

He pushed it into her uncooperative hands and she

stared down at it for a while. As soon as she put on these rings she would be accepting the fate he had decided for her. She would be acceding to his plans. She wasn't ready for that yet.

'Open it!'

She blinked, her senses snapping to attention with his abrupt command. Yet his dark eyes spoke to her on a different level. They contained no anger. Instead they encouraged her to do as he asked, beseeching her to trust him.

Reluctantly she took one end of the immaculate ribbon tie and tugged, letting the bow fall apart. She slid the ribbon off and lifted off the lid. Thick tissue paper covered whatever was inside. She looked up at him, questioning, but his eyes gave no answers, instead urging her on.

She peeled back the thick layers of tissue and gasped.

The paperweight!

The heart-shaped crystal glowed blood red against its white-tissue background, the natural light heightening its lustre while at the same time accentuating its shadows. She lifted it from the box, feeling its smooth weight in her hands, running her fingers over its sensually rounded surface. It was the most beautiful thing anyone had ever given her.

And Paolo had been the one to give it to her.

She smiled and lifted it with both hands, holding it close to her chest. 'Thank you,' she said. 'It's beautiful.'

The sides of his mouth turned up and he nodded. *'Buono,'* he said. 'I'm glad.'

And it seemed the most natural thing in the world

then, with his eyes, rich and warm, looking down on her, to reach up and kiss his cheek, an innocent gesture of thanks. Except that at the last second he moved and it wasn't his cheek her lips found under them, but his mouth, warm and supple and electric.

The carriage rocked to a standstill, breaking them apart, and she looked around, dazed. They were back in the queue of horses alongside the kerb, their ride over.

The driver stashed the reins and jumped down, pulling open the carriage door and smiling up at them both.

'Well, how did you enjoy that?'

She smiled a little self-consciously in return, replacing the paperweight into its box before taking his proffered hand. 'Thank you, that was wonderful. Something I've always wanted to do.'

'Ah, there's a certain magic about it,' he said, tipping his head to his finger as he helped her down.

CHAPTER SIX

His mother was waiting for them. The moment the car pulled up outside the columned portico of the gracious villa the front door swung open and an elegantly dressed woman appeared on the top step. Helene twisted the unfamiliar rings on her finger, drawing in a fortifying breath as she registered the resemblance immediately.

It had to be Carmela Mancini. Paolo's mother. Even though the woman's build was tiny when compared to his powerful frame, they shared the same luscious dark eyes, framed with the same thick lashes.

'*Casa benvenuta,*' she said, her generous mouth smiling as her arms stretched out in greeting. 'Welcome to you both.'

'*Mamma,*' Paolo said, bestowing a kiss on each cheek, 'this is Helene.'

'It's a pleasure to meet you, Signora Mancini.'

The older woman took Helene's hands in her own and squeezed them tight, her eyes narrowing, evaluating even as her smile genuinely bid her welcome.

'So this is the woman who has finally turned my son from a bachelor into a family man.' She nodded. 'I can see why he would be so impatient to marry you even though—' she winked at Helene, her smile broadening as her nod turned into a shake '—I cannot believe my thoughtless son would not even allow his poor mother to be there for the wedding.'

'*Mamma!*' Paolo scolded.

Helene knew she was only half joking. She would have to be made of iron not to have been hurt by her exclusion from the wedding Paolo claimed had been performed in New York. In normal circumstances a wedding would be a celebration for the entire family, not something to where the bride and groom sloped away as if ashamed.

'I'm sorry it happened the way it did, Signora Mancini,' she said sincerely, 'but it was all such a rush.'

That much at least was the truth.

'I understand.' Carmela stroked the younger woman's hands before slipping her arm under Helene's and tugging her towards the house. 'I was once young and impetuous. And, of course, I forgive you, given that you have brought me such wonderful news. It is much too long since we have had a *bambino* in the house. Maria's two children are growing up too fast.' She turned to Paolo misty-eyed, touching his cheek. 'Your father would be so proud of you, I know.'

She sucked in a deep breath and blinked her eyes rapidly, smiling to cover her brief display of weakness.

'But you must both be tired after your long journey. Come inside and rest.'

Helene allowed herself to be led inside the house, feeling as if she'd just passed some sort of test. Carmela had been searching for something in her face, she was sure of it. And she didn't seem half as protective of her son or unwelcoming of her as she'd expected. Was his mother just so happy to see her son married that she was prepared to overlook the rushed circumstances of their marriage or did she suspect that things were not quite how Paolo had explained?

Whatever, it was a welcome surprise for her Milan homecoming. It was clear already that they would get along.

She looked over his mother's dark head across to him, smiling, wondering if he was as relieved as she was with how the introduction had gone, but when her eye caught his she was just about stopped in her tracks. Because it wasn't pleasure she saw there. There was none of the relief she was feeling, none of the satisfaction. Instead every angle and plane of his face was set to accentuate the message coming from his eyes. Anger.

She turned her face away. What had she done now?

She hadn't even made it under the covers. She'd clearly been so tired she'd just taken off her jacket and kicked off her shoes, leaned back into the pillows and fallen fast asleep. And she'd even chosen the smallest bedroom in their allotted suite to do it. She'd gone up to bed hours before him and when he'd finally left to join her he hadn't found her in the suite's main bedroom at all. Instead, here she was, tucked away like some nanny or maid in one of the minor bedrooms.

Was she hiding from him? Was she so anxious to avoid him that she thought she could evade his reach for the next six months by choosing another bedroom from his?

Not a chance.

He looked down at her, her face at rest, her mouth

slightly open, her hair floating out around her head on the pillow.

He reached out one hand, tracing the tips of his fingers over one coiling loop. So soft. He remembered how it felt against his face, its heavy weight smelling of fruit and summer, and he longed to bury his face in it again.

And he would, just as soon as the doctors assured him it was all right. He pulled his hand away, taking in the rest of her, still dressed in her knitted top and fitted trousers.

She couldn't sleep like this, fully clothed on top of the bed. And if he was going to get her under the covers... Blood crashed loud in his ears at his next thought.

He would have to undress her.

For months he'd thought about doing just that. And yet now the opportunity had presented her to him on a plate, he could do nothing more than that. Tomorrow she would see the doctor. Tomorrow he would know. Until then he would have to wait. But that didn't have to stop him from wanting to make her more comfortable.

She would probably stir anyway while he slipped off her clothes. That was a risk he was prepared to take. She looked so deeply asleep it would be cruel to wake her just to make her get changed for bed. And it wouldn't take him long.

He pulled down the covers on the other side of the bed so it was ready for her, then he knelt down alongside and, watching her shuttered eyes for any flickering movements, took hold of the tab on the side closure of her trousers. Holding his breath, he eased down the zipper. Her slow, even breathing hitched only the slightest amount and she moved a fraction, just enough to make the sides of the opening pull apart. A tiny sliver of creamy skin down to her thigh, punctuated by a mere ribbon of lace, met his gaze and he swallowed, suddenly aware of his parched throat.

The dream was back. The dream she'd had time and again since that night in Paris, and this time it felt more real than ever. But this time she was determined her night-time lover wouldn't escape with the dawn light, except she was so tired, her limbs too heavy to lift, and her spirit only too willing to accept the ministrations that soothed and massaged and comforted.

She felt his hands at her waist, peeling away her clothes and easing her to one side so they would slide right off. The air was cool against her legs until she felt his hand, lightly skimming the surface of her skin from her waist right down to her toes, and warmth bloomed under his touch.

His hands scooped under her top, rising up under her arms. She dropped an elbow and he slipped off first one sleeve, then the other. Like a breath of wind she felt the garment lifted over her head and eased away. Fingers traced the lines of her ribs, circling her waist, rounding her back, a massage that simultaneously soothed and stimulated.

She wanted to reach for him; she wanted to hold him in her arms and pull him to her for a kiss. But her arms were so heavy, so lethargic. And she knew that there was no one there and that if she reached for him her dream lover would disappear and she would be left cheated once again.

The clip on her bra dissolved and the straps slid free from her shoulders and for the first time she was sure she heard her dream lover groan. Even in her dream she tingled with anticipation. He wanted her.

Heat focused in her breasts, warmed by a gentle breath—his breath—fanning gently against her peaking flesh. Then his mouth was on her, the soft touch of his lips, the gentle lap of his tongue, to first one nipple, then the other. She arched her back, wanting it to go on; she wanted more of the delicious sensations; she ached for them. But when his lips met her again it was at the skin of her belly, his mouth brushing over the surface in little more than a heated breath. Then his hands were on her thighs, his beautiful long-fingered hands stroking her legs, lower and lower and taking her last remaining garment with them.

She sighed. He could take her now and her dream would be complete. Yet there was nothing more, and she drifted between sleep and dreams and unreality amidst wishes that real life could be so perfect, so gentle and blameless.

Only vaguely she was aware of the sensation of being moved, but she was soon so comfortable, so warmly wrapped in his arms, that it didn't matter.

Her breathing was slow and even again, signalling a return to deep sleep. He envied her. He'd be lucky to sleep at all tonight. The way her body curved luxuriously against his, the neat way she pressed into him in all the right places, the way her natural scent and the fresh smell of her hair coiled into his senses, it was probably madness to hold her this close when his need was so great.

But it had been so long and the torture was worth it to have her in his arms at last.

Even in sleep she'd been so responsive. For a while he'd thought she'd woken, his movements too disturbing, and her flesh so eager, but her tiny sighs were like someone sleep-talking, the breathful murmurs of one in a dream state.

Next time, he promised himself, she would be fully awake. Then she would know it was him and not some fantasy. She would watch him as he made love to her. He wanted her eyes open. He wanted to look into their cool green depths when he entered her. He wanted to see them explode when she came apart in his arms.

He sighed, praying as he clamped his eyes shut that the doctor would have good news for him when he took Helene in to see him in the morning. Until such time as he had the go-ahead to assuage this throbbing need, he would have to ignore it. He could stand one night of torture if he had six months of hot nights to look forward to.

But would six months be enough?

He shoved the thought back from where it had come. It would have to be.

He would make sure it was.

Helene drifted in and out of sleep, coming ever closer to waking before briefly slipping back into her comfortable dream state, easing herself into wakefulness like the tide creeping further up the shore with every lapping wave. Warmth surrounded her, encased her—pinned her down.

Her eyes opened suddenly at the unfamiliar weight, blinking, focusing on the grey light of a room laser-lit with tiny needles of light that eluded the otherwise blackout curtains. Holding her breath, she heard the unmistakable sound of someone breathing behind her.

Paolo.

She tensed and the arm over her shifted slightly, curled fingers brushing against her naked skin.

Naked?

Her senses kick-started into life. She couldn't remember getting into bed, let alone taking her clothes off. And she definitely had no recollection of Paolo joining her.

A wave of panic prickled over her. What else didn't she remember?

Snatches of a dream swirled around in her mind. Like random snapshots from a scene they teased her, refusing to come to order, making no sense. She'd dreamed of Paolo again, only this time it had seemed so real. Snippets of sensation came back to her—her clothes peeling away, a gentle hand gliding over her skin, a warm mouth at her breast.

And like a bolt of electricity, it hit her. She hadn't been dreaming at all. But what concerned her the most was what she couldn't remember. What else had he done? Her mind rewound her dreams in a desperate search for answers. Surely she would remember if he had made love to her? And yet there was nothing, no memory, no musky scent of lovemaking, no physical reminders of any kind.

So why was he here?

Nothing made sense.

He hadn't touched her since his reappearance in New York. And while his control over her life had become an all-pervasive thing, he'd kept his distance from her physically, his eyes only once or twice betraying a hint of memory as to what had happened between them. Which made perfect sense. That night in Paris had been an aberration for them both. He saw her only as a vessel for his baby. An incubator.

An incubator destined for the scrap heap as soon as this child was born.

So what was he doing in her bed now? What did it mean?

And why was every cell of her body on high alert? The skin under his arm tingled, setting off charges that sent out sparks like the sparklers she remembered holding as a child on Guy Fawkes night. Only these sparks relayed through her body, making every part of her exquisitely aware of his naked proximity.

His heat warmed the bed, his heat seeped under her skin, warming her blood.

He shifted alongside her and she held her breath, wondering how she was going to edge out from under his arm without disturbing him further and where she might find her robe when she managed to escape.

His hand slid over her waist, his fingers spreading over the swell of her hip, squeezing slightly, and she jumped involuntarily.

'You slept a long time,' he said. 'You must have been very tired.'

His voice was pure early-morning husky and its throaty edge snagged into her feminine senses like a dose of pure testosterone. She didn't have to turn over to know how he would look; his voice carried with it the visual. His dark eyes would be hooded, slumberous, and his jaw would be shadowed with stubble.

She knew *exactly* how he would look.

All masculine.

Incredibly sexy.

And way too dangerous.

'What happened to my clothes?' she asked, without lifting her head from the pillow and trying to sound as if it was the first thing she said every morning when there was a man in her bed who hadn't been there the night before. 'Who undressed me?'

'I did,' he responded. 'Is that a problem?'

She licked her lips. 'What do you think?' she said, realising her attempt to put him on the defensive had failed miserably and wishing she'd never asked the question at all.

His hand slipped away as the bed moved and she sensed him rise up on one elbow. 'Look at me,' he said.

Wavering, she hesitated. 'Why?'

'Just look at me.'

Keeping the bedclothes tightly wrapped around her, she eased herself over until she was facing him. He looked just how she'd imagined, except his shadowed jaw was set and tight, his eyes more determined than ever.

'You have no need of all this,' he said, indicating the tangle of bedclothes pulled up tight. 'I've seen it all before. And I saw everything last night. You have no secrets from me.'

Heat flooded her cheeks. 'What gives you the right?'

'I am your husband!'

'That's a joke!' But she couldn't argue with him lying down. Pulling the covers with her, she backed herself up against the headboard.

'You're my gatekeeper. You're my jailer. You've locked me up here until I deliver you your child. But as for being a husband? I don't think so. I don't think you know the meaning of the word.'

Skin pulled taut over the bones in his face and his nostrils flared over lips drawn tight.

'In the eyes of the law I am your husband and I—'

'Then the law is a joke!'

'Maybe that's true,' he said with barely controlled fury, 'but that doesn't change anything. I am your husband and I will undress you if I see fit.'

'And am I to believe that that's all you did?' She'd said the words before she realised that she'd given too much away. That she'd shown that she even cared.

Something in his eyes flickered, but not with amusement, despite the curved set of his mouth. 'Would it matter?'

'Of course it would matter! I was asleep. You would have been taking advantage of me.'

His eyebrows lifted and this time he did look amused. 'Don't you think it's a little late to be worried about your virtue? Some might even conclude you are the one taking advantage of me. You were the one who claimed to be protected, were you not?'

'It's not like that!' she insisted. 'You didn't even bother to even ask until we'd had sex that first time and it may already have been too late. And I didn't *claim* to be protected. I believed I was safe and that's what I told you. But none of that is relevant anyway. None of that gives you free access to my body now.'

'You didn't seem to object to the prospect of making love with me last night. On the contrary, you seemed quite accommodating.'

'We didn't—'

His eyes told her nothing. They were blank of emotion, dark windows to nowhere.

'Unfortunately not,' he said, turning away. 'We didn't. But you would have. I have no doubt of that.'

'No,' she insisted emphatically, shaking her head, even though the memories of her dream told her she was kidding herself. 'Look, Paolo, this isn't fair. Isn't it enough that you lock me up here until I have your child? I didn't realise you expected to sleep with me as well. I didn't realise you expected...' Her words trailed off.

'We are married,' he said, throwing back the covers and rising from the bed unashamedly naked, 'whether or not I have any concept of what a husband is. And we are good together in bed. We might as well make the most of it while you're here.'

His callous words fell like acid rain on her heart. He couldn't be that insensitive, that cruel. To use her for sex while she was just about his prisoner and then discard her when he had no more use for her? It was too much. It was too hurtful. He couldn't mean it.

She wanted to drag her eyes away from his naked body as he padded across to the adjoining bathroom—it would be some kind of protest at least. It would show she didn't care, that his body held no attraction for her.

But she couldn't. The magic of his predator-like stride, the beauty of his perfect form, the sheer size of that which made him man—there was no dragging her eyes away, just as she knew there was no denying the fundamental truth of what he'd said.

They had been good together.

They could be again.

But why should it be only on his terms?

She gulped in air as an idea formed in her mind. Maybe there *was* a way to make this work, to bring Paolo closer to her.

Maybe she didn't have to fight him.

Resolve flowed through her veins, warm and reassuring and edged with hope. He didn't have any concept of what he was letting himself in for. He had no idea of the tool he'd just handed her.

Because what he wanted from her, she could use to reach him.

She'd reached him that night in Paris; there was no doubt of that. Otherwise he'd never have bothered to look her up when he was in New York. That first night together in her apartment he'd been in torment, suffering the loss of Sapphy, battling his feelings of guilt, and she'd shared in that pain, and together they'd found a way of dealing with it, a way of blotting it out, at least temporarily.

And now they had more than just a tired wedding contract to bind them together. Now they'd created a life. A child's life.

So could she reach him again? Could their lovemaking make a difference to his attitude?

It had to. Because the man she knew as Paolo couldn't be gone. He'd saved her from a marriage against her will; he'd stood up to one of the most powerful men in the oil world for her, and there was no way he could have changed that much. Because he was a man of integrity, a man who held intense passion for wanting what was right.

That Paolo might be hard to find right now, he might be elusive, but he was still there, buried somewhere beneath the layers of hurt and loss. He had to be.

And maybe, just maybe, if she could find a way to uncover the real Paolo, there was a chance for them all.

CHAPTER SEVEN

THE sound of children's laughter greeted them on their return from the clinic, signalling the arrival of Paolo's sister, Maria, her husband and two children for lunch. Carmela had apparently planned quite a feast and already fabulous aromas were wafting from the large kitchen.

Carmela rushed out and greeted them, asking after the baby in a torrent of kisses and words.

'Buono,' Paolo answered for her as he embraced his mother. 'Things could not be better.'

Helene stole a glance at him. He'd pointedly asked the doctor when it would be safe for them to resume sexual relations despite Helene's obvious embarrassment at his line of questioning. His control last night had suddenly made sense. It wasn't out of concern for her sleeping state that he'd not gone further than he had. He hadn't wanted to harm the baby.

But now that he'd received the answer he'd wanted, how soon before he took advantage of it?

Tonight?

She had to focus on appearing normal, on greeting his younger sister and her husband and their two young children, Vincenzo and Annabella, on listening to what they said and saying the right thing in return. But how could she even pretend to be normal when her body was making preparations for an entirely different kind of celebration?

106

Paolo swung a giggling Vincenzo up onto his shoulders and looked around, and as his eyes met hers she felt it. Desire reached out from their dark depths, telling her that he was thinking the same thing.

Definitely tonight.

She turned her eyes away, but that didn't stop the heat spiralling deep inside. Despite the harsh words they'd exchanged this morning, it didn't stop the anticipation.

She tried to tell herself that her excitement had something to do with the chance to put her scheme into action, but she knew she was lying. Her excitement had everything to do with knowing that he wanted her—that she wanted him. Her excitement was nothing more than primal.

After lunch Helene found herself banished from the kitchen, ordered to relax by both the Mancini women and the housekeeper. She wandered out to the patio, following the sounds of laughter and happy squeals. Carlo leaned against the balustrade smoking a cigarette, laughing at Paolo on all fours on the grass below offering pony rides to Vincenzo and Annabella in turn.

Vincenzo at four was supremely brave and clearly fancied himself as cowboy. Paolo accommodatingly bucked and reared, giving the boy the ride of his life.

At just two Annabella was more hesitant, and content to let her favourite uncle walk her around the grass.

'He's very good with the children,' Helene said, coming up alongside Carlo.

'Paolo will make a great father,' the handsome Italian said reassuringly. 'For a long time he has seemed like a man who hungered for a family. We thought he might marry before now, but somehow he's never seemed able to take that final step.' He turned to her and smiled. 'Until you came along.'

Helene somehow dredged up her own smile in response before looking away, too uncomfortable to try to respond. They'd all expected Paolo to marry Sapphire. He didn't have to say her name for Helene to know that was whom he was thinking about. They'd been a couple for longer than two years. The gossip columns had had them all but married off. The family must have thought their engagement was imminent, and then Sapphire was gone and suddenly a pregnant Helene was on the scene, the new Signora Paolo Mancini.

None of them had any idea of the truth, of the real reason why he'd never married Sapphire or anyone else, why he'd never started a family earlier. Helene had made that impossible.

Would his family resent her for what she'd cost him, the same way Paolo did? Would they support him in his plan to keep the child and set her adrift because of it?

Maybe they would. Unlike her own circumstances, family for the Mancini's seemed paramount. The feeling she had with them was like being wrapped in a giant, soft duvet, surrounded by security, cheered by warmth. But then, if they learned that she'd caused him such long-term heartache—maybe they would think she deserved all he gave her.

She shivered.

'You should relax,' Carlo said, obviously sensing something in her face and drawing his own conclusions. 'Yes, the news of your marriage and the baby was sudden and took us all by surprise, but it is good news for the family and very good news for Paolo. He looks happier than I've seen him in years.'

He did? She looked over to where Paolo had collapsed onto his back on the lawn, the two children climbing and tumbling over him, his rich, deep laughter ringing out between the giggles and squeals, and her heart squeezed tight.

In a year or two their own child might be doing the same thing, playing rough-house with his or her *papà* on the lawn. Would she be here to see it? To witness her child's delight?

She wanted so much to be. Why should he be so anxious to be rid of her? There was still so much she didn't understand about him.

'What happened to Paolo's father?' she asked at last. 'Paolo won't talk about him and I don't feel I can ask Maria or her mother.'

Carlo dragged deeply on his cigarette before flicking it into a nearby ashtray. 'No. They feel his loss greatly still. He died just before Vincenzo was born. We named him for his grandfather.'

'What happened?'

'He had cancer, very seriously. He had operations to remove the malignancy; he had chemotherapy and then radiotherapy. It was one thing after another and then the process started again. He was sick for many years, fighting the disease, Carmela by his side tirelessly supporting him. It was a very difficult time.'

'But ultimately it killed him?'

He leaned down, resting his arms on the balustrade as he watched Paolo with the children. 'Not at all.

After years of struggle he finally beat the disease. The doctors announced he was in remission. Everyone was very excited. The whole family was here to celebrate, cousins, uncles, friends, friends of friends. Paolo flew back from a case he was working on in Germany specially to be part of the celebration.'

He paused and she waited, knowing in her heart that this story did not have the happy ending one would normally associate with overcoming such a heinous disease, not wanting to hear what he had to say next, but knowing that she must.

'Paolo never got to see his father. After spending years overcoming the disease and winning back his life, Vincenzo lost it in a fraction of a second on the *autostrada*. An out-of-control truck hit his car. He didn't stand a chance.'

'Oh, my God,' she said, horrified. 'How terrible for Vincenzo, for everyone.'

'It was worst for Paolo,' Carlo continued. 'His father had planned on surprising him by showing him how much he'd recovered. He was on his way to collect him from the airport when the accident happened.'

She shuddered. It was too horrible to imagine. What should have been a happy homecoming had turned into a shocking tragedy.

Carlo shrugged, crossing his arms as he leaned back on the balustrade, though she could see the harsh lines in his face as he remembered that time. It was clear Vincenzo's death had exacted a terrible toll on the entire family, even for those not directly related by blood.

'Paolo took it badly. They'd always been close, but

now he felt cheated. Just when he was about to have his father back, he was stolen away. Of course he blamed himself. If his father hadn't been driving to collect him, then the accident would never have happened.'

Stolen!

Her blood ground to an icy halt as suddenly everything that was happening made sense. He'd lost his father, stolen from him in the blink of an eye when he'd fought and won the battle to defeat the cancer that had ravaged him.

Barely over that and he'd lost Sapphire, stolen by Khaled, the man who had sworn revenge against him for marrying Helene.

It all made such perfect and ghastly sense.

He'd lost his father and then he'd lost his lover in short order. No wonder he was so determined not to lose his child. No wonder he was so desperate to control her life.

He was a man who had lost far too much already.

Could she really make up for any of that in just a few short months? Would she really be able to give him something back that would help ease all that he had lost and all that she had cost him?

She wanted to try.

She needed to try.

The future of all of them depended on it.

Paolo stood up, a child held in each arm, telling them in their own language that they had worn him out and that he was taking them to their *papà*. But as he looked up towards the balcony it wasn't his brother-in-law his eyes snagged on.

She stood there leaning against the balustrade, her

wavy hair turned to spun gold by the sunlight, the skirt of her short dress floating around her legs. Like a fair-skinned goddess, a bright light amongst his dark-haired, olive-skinned family. She'd been watching him, her green eyes layered with emotions he couldn't guess at. What was she thinking? Why was she watching him?

Need stirred inside him at the vision she made, need that had been making itself felt ever since seeing the specialist that morning. Even the pranks and energy of two small children could not quell the rush of blood he felt at every thought of what he was going to do tonight—at the thought of what he was hungry enough to do right now.

But she'd been so angry this morning, so outraged at the prospect that they should share a bed for more than just sleep, that there was little chance she would be waiting for the same opportunity he was. And yet there was something about the way she looked— something that told him that she wanted more than to argue with him right now.

The pale skin at her throat begged to be kissed, the soft, taunting fabric of her skirt pleaded to be pushed aside so his hands could sweep upwards over the smooth skin of her thighs, to where her liquid heat could wrap itself around him and he could bury himself deep inside her. And the way she was looking at him...

Carlo's voice intruded on his thoughts. The children in his arms were squirming for release.

'Paolo,' he said, laughing, as if this wasn't the first time he'd tried to get his attention. 'Let the children down. *Nonna* has *gelati* for them.'

'Gelati!' they squealed as one. He set them down and they took off into the house, Vincenzo going like a rocket, Annabella toddling along behind with her father as fast as her short legs would allow.

He watched them go before he looked back at Helene. Without saying a word he devoured the few short steps leading up to the patio to where she stood, following his progress through eyes that were slightly lowered, the fingers of one hand toying with her necklace.

He lowered himself the few inches to the balustrade alongside her so that they were almost eye to eye. Her lips parted slightly and he watched the pink tip of her tongue appear then retract, leaving a film of moisture over her top lip. He wished he could have thought of something appropriate to say, but he couldn't speak, couldn't find the words, when all he wanted was to mimic the action of her tongue and moisten her lips himself.

'They're beautiful children,' she said after a little while. 'And they obviously love their *gelati*.'

'All children love ice cream,' he said. 'Do you want some? I'm sure *Nonna* has enough for an entire army of Mancini adults as well as children.'

She shook her head, making the soft, waving tendrils around her face bounce and spring, as if they had a life of their own.

'No,' she said on a breath. 'Do you?'

He reached out a hand and tucked one of the loose tendrils behind her ear. He saw her sharp intake of breath, he witnessed the movement in her throat when she swallowed, but he didn't take his hand away. He left it there, his fingers gently stroking the downy softness of the curve of her ear.

'What I want right now isn't ice cream.'

Her eyes slid sideways to meet his. 'What…? What do…?' She stopped and looked away, as if uncertainty had eaten her words.

'What do I want?' he prompted. His hand slid through her heavy hair, weaving his fingers around and between and dragging the thick streams of hair, exerting just enough pressure to turn her head towards his.

Her eyes dropped to his lips—uncertain, then expectant—and he smiled.

She had to know what he wanted, but that still wasn't going to stop him telling her. With both hands he drew her around, hauling her in closer to him. And when his lips were but a fraction away from hers, when he could feel her warm breath mingling with his, her soft breath on his skin, her soft hair curling into his cheek, he told her.

'I want you.'

CHAPTER EIGHT

PAOLO felt the shudder move through her as his lips meshed with Helene's, supple and pliant and slightly parted, as if she was ready. As if she was anticipating his kiss. And that knowledge fuelled his desire. He breathed her in, her taste and scent tangling together with warmth and need, and he steered her closer, drawing her in between his legs as his kiss deepened.

Her mouth opened at his coaxing and the liquid heat of her welcomed him inside. She tasted so sweet, so compulsively addictive, and his thoughts turned to hopes of another invitation, a deeper taste of heaven that beckoned as he held her so close against his aching hardness that she could not mistake his intention.

She didn't, if her subtle movements were any indication, her hips between his thighs, her breasts firm where they brushed against his chest. But, whilst subtle, their effect on his body was anything but. Every pulse of her body, every tiny shift in her position was enough to make him want to act on his desires.

His hands ached to pull up the skirt of her dress and clamp down on her bare flesh; his mouth yearned to seek the hard points of her breasts that butted into his chest and drag them into his mouth. But this was not the place. As much as he wanted to keep going, as much as he wanted to follow this beginning to its logical conclusion, they couldn't stay here. Any moment the children could return.

On a ragged breath he dragged his mouth from hers.

Her eyes were bright and luminous, her lips plumped and lush, and it was anguish to tear himself away.

'Did you have plans for this afternoon?' he asked, knowing he'd never make it if he had to wait until tonight.

The green lights in her eyes sparked with passion. 'I do now.'

His growl was tinged with victory as he swung her into his arms, his mouth meeting hers once more in a silencing kiss. Her weight was nothing in his arms. She curved against him, not fighting, her limbs settled around him like liquid, her breasts crushed into his chest.

As soon as they were alone he would pull back the fabric that covered them. He longed to fill his hands with their weight. He longed to take their pebbled peaks in his mouth once more. Last night had been a taste. Today would be the feast.

Footprints alerted him to the fact they weren't alone and he cursed that he hadn't already made his escape. He lifted his head to see two small children, their chocolate-smeared faces seriously studying whatever he was doing with their new aunt.

Helene turned her head at the intrusion, and smiled when she saw their faces, her lilting laughter nowhere near soothing the raw edge of his desire. She straightened up in his arms, gesturing that he should let her down. Slowly, reluctantly, he complied, allowing her legs to slide gently to the ground. But he maintained his proprietary hold on her shoulders.

'What are they saying?' she asked Paolo, after Vincenzo junior had rattled off something, promising herself she would start to work on her Italian as soon as possible so she could better communicate with them all.

Paolo sighed. 'I promised to take them swimming in the pool after lunch. I had forgotten.'

The two children looked so hopeful and yet so forlorn that their uncle might have changed his mind.

'Then you must. Come on. Last one in is a rotten egg.'

They didn't understand her words, but it didn't matter because they picked up on her enthusiasm. In a few minutes they were all changed and splashing together in the crystal-clear water of a pool set skilfully into part of the terrace where the land sloped away, providing views over the surrounding countryside that seemed to go for ever.

Annabella sat in a blow-up duck, floating and kicking herself along happily on the surface. The young Vincenzo was eager to display his already advanced swimming skills and challenged anyone and everyone to a race.

They spent a good hour in the pool with them both. Afterwards Carmela came with refreshments and Helene dried off in a lounger with her, taking in the view over the landscape spread out beyond, while Maria took her worn-out daughter off for a bath, Vincenzo following reluctantly on their heels.

She sipped on her ice, watching Paolo churning up and down the now-quiet pool, his gleaming muscles pumping hard, water alternately sliding over and then sluicing off his streamlined body as his arms powered through the water. She'd lost count of the number of laps he'd completed of the long pool, but he must have swum kilometres already and still he showed no signs of easing off.

Carmela offered the jug of soda and she held out her glass for a refill.

'It seems my son has the devil at his heels,' the older woman said. 'Even when he relaxes he seems driven.'

Helene looked over at her, wondering if there was more to her words than first appeared, but Carmela was contemplating the contents of her glass, swirling the icy mixture around.

'I notice he plays to win,' Helene offered. 'Whatever he does.'

The older woman nodded. 'That's so true. In that way he's very much like his father was. There was nothing his father couldn't do once he set his mind to it...' She looked away, over into the distance, and Helene knew that she was thinking that all the determination in the world hadn't been able to save him from such a pointless death.

'You must miss him terribly.'

She nodded and turned her head back, her eyes sheened with moisture. 'I feel bad that he's missed out on meeting his grandchildren. He was so looking forward to Maria's first child. I know he would have loved them all so much.'

Carmela took a sip in the ensuing silence, visibly collecting herself. 'But it's the present we have to focus on and we have so much to look forward to now.' She reached across and took Helene's hand. 'I'm so glad that Paolo has found you. He seemed so lost for so long—so unsure of his place in the world even as he was making a success of it.'

She smiled and squeezed her hand. Helene battled to return the gesture, the enormity of what she'd cost Paolo only now sinking in, when she had the chance to hear from his family how twelve years of being tied to her had affected him. It was more than just the cost of losing him Sapphire; it was what he had been denied all that time, the uncertainty, the inability to make his own life.

And he'd done that for her. For a promise made when he'd been barely twenty years old. And he'd stuck by that promise no matter what it had cost him.

'Your son is a good man, Carmela.'

'I know. And I know you will make him very happy. A child is just what he needs to give his life focus.'

They both turned back to watch Paolo, still churning through the water, his body sleek and arrow-straight. Helene couldn't look at him without thinking about what they might have been doing if they hadn't been interrupted with this swimming session.

All that energy, all that intensity... His long arms, those strong legs would be right now tangled with hers. Those narrow hips, now encased so enticingly in black trunks, could be pressing against her, his endless power surging into her.

Despite the warmth of the afternoon sun she shivered involuntarily, aware of nerve endings under her blue and white patterned one-piece prickling into awareness again.

Oh, Lord, she only had to look at him to get ideas.

'What about your parents, Helene? Are they excited? I hope they're not too disappointed that we've stolen you away to live with us.'

She blinked and stared at her glass, thinking that the ice came a poor second to the subject of her parents for cooling her heated thoughts.

'I'm not sure they'd even care,' she began, then wondered how to finish when she noticed Carmela's look of shock. 'My parents have had nothing to do with me since I was seventeen.'

'Oh, but that is terrible. How could they do such a thing to you? And how could they not want to know about such a wonderful thing?'

'Carmela,' she said, trying to calm the older woman, 'it's okay, really. I disagreed with something they wanted me to do and—'

'What did they want you to do?' she demanded.

'They arranged for me to marry the son of a business partner of my father's as part of their deal. I refused.' She hesitated, wondering how much she could tell, but there was no need to bring Paolo into this. It was not her place to reveal his truth. 'So I ran away.'

'Oh, but of course you did!' Carmela sighed, reaching over to stroke Helene's hand. 'So you have no family in England? No family anywhere?'

Her teeth bit down on the inside of her lip as she shook her head.

'Then it is right that you are here. We will look after you.' She moved across to embrace the younger woman. 'This is your home now. We are your family.'

Tears pricked at her eyes and she smiled, warmth filling her heart. 'Thank you,' she whispered as she hugged the woman back, trying to force away the tightness in her throat. She'd always managed by herself; she'd made a success of her life by herself; she'd told herself time and again that she needed no one. And yet Carmela's generous words touched her on a level she'd thought long dead.

To belong to a family—a real family. It was more than she could ever have hoped. Paolo's plans for her might not be long-term, her own plans to win him might not be successful, but she had been welcomed into this family and it felt so good.

'You don't know how much that means to me.'

Carmela patted her on the back. 'It's an honour to have you as part of our family. Now I'm going inside to check if Maria needs help with the children.'

'Can I do anything?'

'No,' she said, urging her to stay seated when she'd tried to rise. 'We promised the children a visit to the market. You stay and relax, but make sure you take care—your skin is far too precious for our sun.' She gave her a quick kiss on the cheek and a promise to be back later that afternoon before heading off towards the house.

'That sounded cosy.'

His voice sliced through her warm feelings like a scythe. Paolo was standing at the shallow end of the pool, water running from his gleaming body in rivulets. He tossed back his head, flicking the moisture from his dark hair in drops that shone like jewels in the sun while his hand followed the action, raking back his sodden hair into some sort of order. If he was breathless from his exertions, the gentle rise and fall of his glimmering chest gave no indication.

She swallowed. She had no idea how much he'd heard, but she was damned sure she'd said nothing that he could be angry about.

'Your mother is very kind.'

'Don't get too close to her. I don't want her hurt.'

With a push he hoisted himself straight out of the pool and onto his feet.

'How would I hurt her?'

'When you leave.'

When she left. Of course. After Carmela's warm words, Paolo's reminder came like a dose of ice.

'I see,' she said, sitting up in her chair as pieces of the puzzle fell into place. 'That's what that dark look was yesterday when we arrived—you were warning me off. You don't want me getting too friendly with your mother.'

'Exactly,' he said, picking up a towel to blot his face.

'So I take it you'd rather I was rude to your mother—that way she'll be happy when I leave. Is that it?'

'Don't be ridiculous,' he said, tossing the towel away. 'Just keep your distance.'

'Which was no doubt your cunning reason for bringing me here, I guess,' she said, her voice heavily laced with sarcasm. 'So I could keep my distance. Who would have picked that?'

She stood up to move away from the chair, but her path was blocked by six feet two of scowling Italian testosterone.

'I brought you here to look after you,' he thundered, his eyes blazing fury, the tendons in his neck stretched tight.

She stared up into his face with a look that would ensure he was one hundred per cent aware of her own anger.

'Then you needn't have bothered,' she said, her teeth barely parting as she let the words fly, 'because I'm perfectly capable of looking after myself.'

Before he had a chance to respond, before waiting for his reaction, she'd stepped around him and dived headlong into the pool. The water hit her like a rush, but it would take more than a drop in the temperature to cool her anger. Paolo wasn't the only one who could take his frustrations out with laps. She started striking out, building up a rhythm, blocking out everything but the feel of propelling herself through the water.

Again and again she turned, lap after lap, revelling in the feeling of moving through a different medium. If only she could negotiate a route as easily through the hazardous depths that made up Paolo. But unlike the pristine water of the pool there was nothing at all clear about him. His emotional landscape was murky and filled with snags that threatened to pull her down whenever she thought she was making progress.

She kept on, ignoring the heavy burn in her arms, forcing them to work, and counting down the strokes until the wall and her next turn.

Except this time something was blocking her way. She saw his legs in front of her, planted wide on the pool's tiled floor. Without breaking her stroke she changed direction to move around the obstacle. Suddenly a hand snared her wrist and stopped her dead. She came up spluttering, trying to wrest her hand away.

'Let me go!' She wanted to shout, but the necessary breath just wasn't there and her words came out a gasping cry of desperation.

'Stop fighting,' he ordered. 'Calm down.'

Now he had both her wrists and there was no way she was calming anywhere. It didn't help that her muscles felt like jelly after her exertions, and without the water to support her she doubted she'd even be able to stand.

'What do you think you're doing?'

'I'm telling you to stop.'

'I don't take orders from you. Let me go!'

She twisted one of her slippery wrists out of his grasp and thrashed out at him, but he moved and her fist slammed into water sending the splash high into his face. Within a second he'd snared the free wrist again. Frantically she bucked against his grip. 'Who the hell do you think you are?' she demanded.

'What are you trying to do? Wear yourself out?'

'Don't pretend to care about me. I know that's a lie.'

'Someone has to look after you.'

'You couldn't give a damn about me!' She spat out the words like machine-gun fire as she fought to free her arms. But this time his grip wasn't giving way; if anything it was edging her towards him, closer to his wall of chest, and he was moving, circling around so that it was becoming more and more difficult to keep herself braced on her feet. She shifted her stance, fighting for purchase as the water swirled between them, trying to maintain her distance from his mus- cled body.

'You only brought me here so you could control

this pregnancy. You don't really want me here and you don't want me getting close to your family. All I am to you is a walking incubator. All you want is this baby!'

'That's where you're wrong.'

'Admit it! It's the truth.'

'You know that's not the whole story,' he said, ceasing his fight, his voice suddenly low and even. 'You know that's not the only reason I want you here.'

She blinked in the sudden stillness, as if taken aback by his sudden change of direction, her eyes wide and questioning.

'You know I want you for much more than that.'

Through parted lips her breathing came fast and shallow as she recovered from both her swimming and the torrent of arguments that had ensued. And maybe they weren't the only reasons. Below her Lycra swimsuit her chest rose and fell rapidly, forcing the clearly outlined shape of her breasts and the peaks of her nipples to his attention. Despite the cool water he felt his own internal heat rising.

He smiled and nodded his head a fraction. 'I see we're on the same wavelength.'

He let go her wrists as his arms circled her hips, taking advantage of her stunned silence to haul her in closer to him.

Her hands braced against his shoulders, her hair curled unchecked, a wild frame around her face where her lips waited, full and quivering.

'Paolo,' she said on a whisper, her voice somewhere between a question and a warning. 'Paolo.'

CHAPTER NINE

Dio! Paolo sucked in a breath. What her voice did to him! It seemed to reach inside and curl its way into his deepest places. He pulled Helene closer against him and it was her turn to gasp when their bodies collided, his hands lifting her higher so that her hips lined up with his and there could be no mistaking his intent.

One hand cemented her to him while the other travelled languorously up the length of her back, to curve around the column of her neck. He felt her skin, moist and supple; he felt the firm press of her body against his; he felt the beat of her heart through his fingertips on her throat. He groaned. It wasn't enough. There was so much more he ached to feel.

He slanted his mouth and meshed his lips with hers. She tasted slightly salty from the pool, and lush and warm, like a siren should taste. She'd coaxed him into the pool as surely as if she'd sat on a rock and sung magic to him, her feminine form a magnet for his eyes, her cool indifference a calculated provocation.

Her mouth opened, blossoming under his, letting him taste more of her, possessing her mouth. As she leant into the kiss her shoulders melted against him and with no difficulty he swept aside the straps of her swimsuit.

Her head pulled out of the kiss despite his resistance. He couldn't lose her now, not when he was so close. Already his plans to have her again had been delayed. If it wasn't enough that he'd had to wait the weeks it took to have the doctor's go-ahead, even today he'd had to grit his teeth against the demands of his family when all he wanted to do was have her alone.

And now he did, there was no way he wanted to stop.

Her eyes looked nervously around, darting from side to side. 'Your family—the children...'

He could have howled with relief. 'Carlo drove them all into town. They won't be back for hours.'

Her focus settled back on him, the green of her eyes reflecting facets of gold in the light that echoed the sun-kissed streaks in her hair. He removed her hands from his shoulders and slipped her one-piece straps down over them. Then he lifted each hand and, without taking his eyes from hers, kissed it solemnly before replacing it around his neck.

'You are so beautiful,' he said. 'You know, I have dreamed of this ever since that night in Paris.'

Her eyes widened, her breath barely a whisper as she gazed up at him.

'Make love with me, Helene.'

For a moment she didn't move, only the staccato pulse in her throat betraying whatever was going on inside her head. Then she tightened the grip around his neck, pulling herself up higher until her lips could reach his, and this time it was her lips issuing the invitation, her tongue seeking entry into his mouth.

He had no intentions of declining. Exhilaration surged in his veins as her passion was given free reign, welcoming his efforts and matching them. They slid into the water, tumbling and rolling under the surface, their mouths locked in a kiss that defied their need to breathe, her hair drifting around them like a sensual cloud.

Then together they broke the surface, gasping for oxygen to further fuel the blaze they had started. This was the woman he knew from Paris; this was what he'd hungered for ever since.

His hands peeled away the rest of her swimsuit and revelled in the touch of her exposed flesh, cupping her breasts, skimming down the curve of her waist to the flare of her hips and her neatly rounded behind. Every part of her was perfect. Every part of her would be his.

Was his.

Heat pooled in his loins and he shucked off his trunks in record time. He angled her into the steps, drifting her back against their support, bracing her in his arms to cushion her skin. Then his mouth could no longer resist what his hands had been rediscovering. Almost reluctantly he dragged his mouth from hers, trailing kisses down the line of her throat and chest, to where the peaks of her breasts broke the surface like sleek white islands, firm and inviting and glossed with moisture.

With a low growl he took the tight bud of one ripe breast into his mouth. He heard her inward rush of air, he felt her body meld to his nuzzling movements and felt himself react in turn.

Her fingers raked the skin at his back and lower, her touch an incendiary to his desire. The arch of her back, the thrust of her hips, everything was right, everything was perfect. Her need fed into his own.

He lifted his mouth and found her other breast, drawing it into his mouth, rolling the rigid peak with his tongue, suckling gently on the tip. He wanted to taste more of her, all of her, but, as on that night in Paris, there was a more pressing compulsion, a more urgent need.

His mouth found hers again, hot and waiting and expectant, the water between them eliminated in a rush in the press of their bodies. She shifted to accommodate him and he slid between her cream-skinned thighs to somewhere he'd longed to be for months. And he wanted to take his time, he wanted to spin out this moment, but there was no way he could, not with her in his arms, in this place where soon they would be joined.

And then anticipation became reality. He entered her slowly at first, testing, teasing, driving them both insane with primitive need before he filled that need with one single, slick thrust that stopped the world as every cell in his body focused on their union. Her muscles tightened around him, welcoming, coaxing as every sensation seemed magnified. He felt her cool skin and her liquid heat; he felt the gentle lap of water at their sides; he saw her hair fanning out like a golden mantilla around her head, he heard his name on her breath.

And as he began to move she responded, their movements a choreographed dance older than time, a rhythm governed by the cosmos.

They took each other there, to the sun and the stars. He felt her come apart with his final thrust, he felt her shatter in his arms and that was all he needed to know as he went with her over the brink.

* * *

The bright afternoon had long turned into the dusky tones of evening before they stirred. They'd moved from the pool eventually, when their breathing had been under control and when their limbs had been able to support them once more, and made it to the showers and then to the master bedroom in their suite. At each stop they had given in to the temptation to make love, as if making up for the months they'd wasted.

She lay with her head on his arm, his face so close to hers that his warm breath skimmed over her like a balm, the heat from his body a glow, filtering its way through her like a heated massage.

He was the most wonderful lover, strong, considerate—she hugged herself with a smile—*insatiable*.

Every muscle hummed with the after-effects of their lovemaking, every part of her had been made love to, felt loved.

She looked up at him, his lids closed, his breath even and steady. He wasn't asleep, she knew, simply dozing as she had been, enjoying the brief peace, the time between sessions. Because they would make love again—she knew it.

But it was more than that. She'd hoped there was a chance to get through to him, to make him realise that she had more to offer him than just a child, that she could be more to him than just a temporary wife. And after today she knew there was that chance.

He hadn't made love to her like a stranger, like a person who meant nothing. There was no way that was possible.

Reaching up, she lightly touched her lips to the corner of his mouth. 'Thank you,' she whispered.

Without opening his eyes, he turned his lips into a lazy smile. 'What was that for?'

'Just…everything,' she said, nestling down again into the crook of his shoulder.

He lifted his head then, rolling her back along his arm and looking down into her face, with his free hand smoothing away the loose drifts of her hair. There were questions in his eyes, then a sudden narrowing.

'Are you all right?'

She blinked. 'I'm fine.'

'I haven't hurt you, or…?'

'Or the baby?' She finished his question for him, feeling her warm inner glow dissipate in the cold reality of his primary concern. But then, she'd known this wasn't a one-shot deal—that she couldn't expect to bring him around to wanting her in just one day. As it was, she hoped six months would be long enough.

'We haven't hurt the baby,' she said. 'I'm sure of it.'

'Then why do you suddenly seem so sad?'

She forced a smile and a low laugh. 'Maybe you just wore me out.'

This time the smile on his face looked positively smug. 'Does that mean you've had enough?'

'Oh, no.' She smiled back, her eyes issuing their own challenge. 'Not a chance.'

'Good,' he announced. 'Because I'm not finished with you yet. Not by a long way.'

He rolled her back over so that now she was sitting

astride him, the evidence of his endless stamina yet again making its presence felt between them.

She swallowed back on a sudden urge of heat as he reached up and took the weight of her breasts in his hands.

'You don't think we should be going down and joining the others?'

'We'll go down,' he said, lifting himself up to take one already tightening peak in his mouth. 'Eventually.'

Paolo's desire showed no signs of waning over the following few days. To all the world they must have looked like true newly-weds, his touch never straying far from her, his eyes always seeking her out across a room. The tension he'd displayed in New York had gone and he actually seemed happier.

He even started drawing her into conversations in the evening when sitting with his mother after dinner.

She'd held back at first, reluctant to contribute to the conversation if it meant incurring his wrath for somehow trying to ingratiate herself with his mother, but he'd insisted on her opinions and their discussions had become a nightly ritual.

During the days he explored the countryside with her. He took her into Milan and showed her around his city like the proud countryman he was. They spent hours in the magnificent Duomo in Milan's central square and she marvelled at the intricate Gothic architecture that had taken five centuries to complete, with its stunning stained-glass windows and thousands of statues. From the roof terraces all of Milan seemed to stretch out before them in a breathtaking view that ended on the nearby snow-capped Bergamo Alps.

Together they toured through the renaissance glory of the Castello Sforzesco and the museums and collections it housed before wandering aimlessly along the streets arm in arm, stopping for pastries and coffee along the way. It was only when they reached the Via Monte Napoleone that Paolo's demeanour suddenly changed and tightness once again pulled the skin of his face achingly tight.

She didn't have to ask. The shopfront heralded the name of its designer in large letters. Bacelli. They were deep in the heartland of fashion design and this was the salon where Sapphire had once worked.

Her heart constricted. She'd known it would take more than sex to make him forget about the pain of losing Sapphire and be willing to accept Helene herself in her place as his life partner. But as the days had passed she'd convinced herself she was making progress. Now just one look at his anguished face told her she had such a long way to go.

'You miss her very much,' she offered as he hustled her past.

He looked down at her, clearly taken aback that she had any concept of what he was thinking. 'I failed her. I as good as delivered her to him on a plate. I can never forgive myself for that.'

His eyes were empty and devoid of hope, open wounds to his hurt, and pain tore through her like a thunderbolt. If he would never forgive himself, how then could he ever forgive her?

That night their lovemaking was different. More tender, more poignant, as if tinged with regret and sorrow for all that had been lost, for all that had been wasted.

She wanted to soothe him with her love, to reach out and absolve him of his guilt and his pain, but he didn't want her love. He never had. The woman he loved, the woman whose love he wanted, was gone, lost to him, and Helene was the one to blame.

So she gave the only thing left to her that he could use—her body—and as he launched himself with her into the abyss she hoped it was enough to keep him.

CHAPTER TEN

'YOU look happy.'

Helene felt Paolo's hands circle her waist and reel her in, his touch drawing her like a magnet. She drew her eyes from the blue waters of the lake and looked back at him. Dressed in his fine Italian knit shirt and dark trousers with the light breeze tugging at the hair at his collar, he looked so good she felt an insane burst of pride.

He might not be hers, but she was with him, and that was enough to draw looks of envy from passing women. Who could blame them?

'How could I not be in a place such as this?'

They both looked out over the view. He'd brought her to Lake Como, just a short journey from his family's villa outside bustling Milan, yet a complete world away from the frenetic pace of the city.

They journeyed around the lake, stopping in the town of Como to take in the view from the Piazza Cavour, and it was another breathtaking view. Ancient villages clung to steep hillsides that plunged into the jewel-like waters of the lake. Lush Mediterranean foliage vied for attention with alpine peaks.

The overall effect was one of tranquillity and peace and it was impossible not to feel good. But there was more to it than that. The past few days he'd made her feel more and more special. Their lovemaking had

135

become more tender, less rushed, and there were times when she thought he must be starting to love her, even just a little.

He spun her around to face him and she caught something fleeting momentarily shadowing his eyes. 'Come,' he said, with his hand at her shoulder. 'Let's find somewhere to eat. We need to talk.'

Apprehension put a sudden halt to her good feelings. They'd been talking for days with hardly an argument between them. Why the cloak of seriousness now?

'About what?' she asked, doing her best to keep her voice light.

Without answering he found them an isolated table at a local trattoria and reeled off an order in Italian before sending the waiter scurrying away.

'What is it you want to talk about?' she prompted.

He leaned back in his chair, his legs stretched in front, his arms wide, and she gained the distinct impression she wasn't about to hear good news.

'The case I was working on in New York—there have been complications—an appeal.' He paused. 'I need to cut short my leave and return to work on the case.'

'But it's your firm! You're the senior partner. Can't they find someone else?'

'There is no one else. I know the case better than anyone. I can't let them down now. We're too close.'

'But you will be working from the Milan office?'

His eyes remained on hers, but there was none of the assurance she wanted. 'Then…?'

'There are times I will have to be in New York. It

is unavoidable. But I will spend as much time as possible based in Milan.'

'I see.' The words were clipped and sharp and she'd meant them to sound that way.

His jaw shifted sideways. 'What do you ''see''?'

'That you can't stand the thought of someone else heading your case. That you're too much of a control freak to let go.'

His sigh was long and spoke volumes as he sat forward in his chair. 'I was hoping you might understand.'

'Of course I understand. You're following a time-honoured tradition, after all.'

His frown joined his heavy brows together. 'Now what are you talking about?'

'It's how every good caveman is supposed to act. First you drag the woman back to your cave to bear your offspring and then you leave her there while you go out slaying dinosaurs.'

'Don't be so melodramatic!'

'I don't believe you're going to do this! You ripped me out of my life and brought me here so you could control me, and now you're taking off for New York again. I don't get it. Are the fees worth that much to you that you can't trust someone else with the case?'

Cold fury tightened the skin of his face and the set of his jaw as he regarded her silently.

She'd made him angry again. What did he expect? But he had no idea what he was really costing her. Because if her plan to make him love her was to have any chance at all, she needed him to be here, she needed to be able to show him how good things could be between them. It was clear that already he'd mellowed these past few days. She was making progress, but she couldn't if he was in New York. They would never bridge their differences that way.

'Maybe I should come with you?' It was the perfect solution. He might have to work long hours, but at least they would have some time together.

'No,' he said, dashing her hopes emphatically. 'You will be better off here.'

'Then what am I supposed to do while you're off lighting up the legal world?'

'Enjoy yourself. Relax.'

'And after I've filed my nails and washed my hair?'

'I am offering you luxury on a plate and you find fault? I'm saying you can spend your days how you see fit—go shopping, visit the sights, laze by the pool if you choose. There are plenty of others who would jump at the chance for such a lifestyle.'

'I can spend my days how I see fit?' Her ears had pricked up with this comment. 'Then I have a better idea,' she said, suddenly leaning forward in her chair. 'I could do project work here, in Milan, for the IBW. There's no need for me to go near an office. I can set something up at the villa, turn one of the smaller bedrooms into an office and have the Bureau send work to me online—'

'No!'

His sharp retort threw her back in her seat. 'But—'

'You do not have to work.'

'I like to work. I'm good at my job—it's important to me.'

'I will not have you working. That was not part of our arrangement.'

'"Our arrangement"? This was never *our* arrangement. It was always what you wanted; you never once considered me.'

'Nevertheless, you will not work.'

'But you'll be working! Why shouldn't I do the same?'

He waved aside her protests with a flick of one wrist. 'It's not an issue we need to discuss.'

'Oh, yes, it damn well is!' Harsh and bitter fury ran in her veins. It was her father again, telling her how to run her life, telling her what she could and couldn't do. 'I need to do something. Maybe my work doesn't seem as earth-shattering as your big-bucks legal business, but the IBW does make a difference to women's lives all over the world and especially in Third World countries. Why shouldn't I be able to keep working while I'm here? What is your problem? Don't you have enough money already?'

His olive skin darkened, a tell-tale pulse at his temple betraying his anger. 'Forget about your job. Right now this baby is your first responsibility.'

She turned away from him, too angry to look in his direction, and wondering if she was ever going to get through to him. But there were no answers in the lively clatter of the restaurant, no solutions that could be plucked out of the air, and she knew in the end she had to face him. 'I want to know,' she said, turning back, 'if you are going to try and control this baby's life like you control mine. Are you going to push it around and tell it what to do? Are you going to make all its decisions for it? Because I feel sorry for the poor child already. You sometimes make me wish there was no baby.'

'I will not let you speak about our child in such a way!'

His words were quietly spoken but intensely felt and she reeled back with their force. Did he think she was wishing away her child? How could he?

Her hand flattened down low on her belly, below where her waist was just starting to noticeably thicken. He might want to run this child's life, but it was still her child—would always be her child, and she would love it for ever.

'I didn't mean...'

'It's too late to wish this all away,' he hissed, cutting her off. 'There is a baby and we're all living with the consequences.'

Aren't we just? she thought mutinously as the waiter arrived with their meals.

'Now that that's settled,' he said, after the waiter had filled their water goblets and departed, 'there's something else I want to discuss with you.'

'It's far from settled, Paolo,' she said, her voice even and firm. 'If you are away in New York, I fail to see how you can stop me working. Besides which, it's the only way I'm going to be able to keep in touch with what's happening at the Bureau. Otherwise I'm going to be hopelessly out of touch with my projects when I go back next year.'

The look he gave her was pure basalt, shiny and hard and the product of some of the world's greatest heat.

'That's what I wanted to talk to you about,' he said. 'You're not going back.'

CHAPTER ELEVEN

'WHAT do you mean?'

'There is no reason for you to go back.'

'But my job...'

'There is a more important job for you here. You will have a child to take care of.'

Helene's heart lurched in a way that sent hope unfurling cautiously within her. But she'd had her hopes raised before, only to be dashed again, and she couldn't let herself get on that emotional roller coaster again.

'You—you want me to stay?' It was almost impossible to get the words out. And it was inconceivable that Paolo's stance would have softened to such an extent that he had changed his mind about her leaving—particularly given the heated discussion of the last five minutes.

'It seems to me,' he started, wishing he'd gone about today's topics entirely differently. He'd known she wouldn't be happy about giving up her work, so why had he mentioned his need to go back to work first? It had only aggravated the situation with her when he needed her to put the baby first if she was to accede to his plan. 'That there's no reason for you to go back to Paris once the child is born.'

Her heart thumped so loud in her chest her words almost tripped over it. 'And...why is that?'

'The child will need you—you should breast-feed.

141

Carmela said so, and Maria, that it is best for the baby.'

'*They* said so.'

Her tone offered him little encouragement, but he wasn't about to give up now.

'You have something against breast-feeding?'

'I never said that.'

He surveyed her face, searching for the truth behind her glinting green eyes and her cool words, but unable to shake the visions that had plagued him ever since his mother had asked him if Helene would feed the baby herself.

Their baby, suckling at Helene's creamy breast, its lips attached firmly to her nipple.

He wanted to see it.

And it made him burn in ways he'd never before imagined. It wasn't about sex, which had surprised him. It was more a strange pull, or an instinctive knowledge that this would be a good thing. The right thing.

He swallowed, dragging his thoughts back to the present. He had to convince her to stay first.

'You do want the best for our child.'

'Of course I do. I have all along.'

'Then stay, and look after the child.'

Her eyes swirled with uncertainty as tiny creases marred the perfect bridge of her nose. What was she thinking? Was she weighing up the baby with her job?

'How long exactly would you require me to breast-feed?'

His jaw clenched, jamming his back teeth together. He was right. Already she was calculating how long she could be away from her work, how far she could extend her leave without jeopardising her position. He blew out on a long breath and recognised his disappointment. Knowing that he was so right about her wasn't the least bit satisfying.

He ran one hand back through his hair.

'Carmela is genuinely fond of you, as are all the family. Already she's grown used to having you around. She would be devastated were you to leave to return to Paris.'

'You told me in New York that she'd get over me.'

He nodded his acknowledgement. 'Even so, it would be hard for her. And for the children. Already they love you as their aunty. Is there any reason to disappoint them?'

Her eyes considered him critically. 'And staying longer will make it easier on them? I don't understand what you're saying, Paolo. What exactly are you proposing? I think you should spell it out.'

'It's quite simple. My family believes we're man and wife and has accepted you into the family. On top of that our first child is due before Christmas.'

'Hang on,' she said, holding up her hand. 'You said "first child".'

Silence slid open between them like a chasm.

'Exactly,' he said at last. 'Whether we like it or not, we're already bound together by this child. Why then shouldn't we use it to our advantage? I want more children.' He shrugged. 'My family likes you. So why shouldn't we stay together? Why shouldn't I have those children with you?'

As little about proposals as Helene knew, she was pretty sure they were supposed to sound warm, and not like something that came gift-wrapped in ice crystals. And yet she must be insane even to hesitate. This was the very thing she'd wanted and hoped would happen, that he would relent from his determination to be done with her as soon as the child was born and ask her to stay with him and the baby. This was exactly what she'd hoped for.

Except, the way she'd planned it, it wasn't intended to be based on her child-rearing capacities, or be done to ensure the minimum of disruption to his family. Her plan had been predicated on him asking her to stay because he would suddenly realise that he wanted her.

That he loved her.

'Let me get this straight,' she started. 'You want to keep this arrangement between us going?'

'It makes sense. The baby will have two parents to grow up with, maybe even brothers and sisters in the future.'

'And you think that would work?'

'Why not? Over the last few weeks you've been happy enough, haven't you? And we've proven how compatible we are.'

'Compatibility in bed is hardly the basis for a permanent relationship.'

'It counts for a lot. Most couples don't have half of what we share.'

Maybe that was true, but didn't he feel anything for her at all? Didn't he want her to stay for what she could give him, and not just for the baby and his family?

She had to know. 'And what about love? Where does that come into it?'

There, she'd said it. She held her breath, not knowing where it would lead—she had no idea how she could confess her love for him even if he demanded to know the truth—but the question was out there between them.

He pushed his barely touched dish away, brushing the napkin across his lips.

'We both know why we're here,' he said. 'If it weren't for this baby, then you would be back in Paris and I would probably never have left New York. I think we both have to be realistic. This isn't a normal marriage by any stretch of the imagination, but I'm prepared to live with that. The question is, are you?'

If it weren't for this baby. Her mind was numb and reeling as his phrases played over and over in her head. *Whether we like it or not, we're already bound together by this child.*

There was no question of him liking it, none at all. That much at least was clear. Without this baby they wouldn't be together at all. It was as simple as that.

Her throat tightened, tinder dry, making it impossible to swallow and yet her glass was near empty. Their heated discussion had turned any lubricating effects of the water to dust.

'So, what's in it for me? Apart from the regular sex, I mean.' She threw out the challenge even while part of her screamed at her to hurl her agreement at him before he changed his mind. After all, she could have him, she could have their child—their children—and she would belong, really belong, in a family for the first time in her life.

She could have exactly what she wanted.

But it wasn't *how* she wanted it.

And it wasn't enough.

His eyes glinted pure heat while a muscle twitched threateningly in his cheek.

He was angry. Good, so the hell was she. She wasn't in the mood to stop now.

'And all it will cost me is to give up my job, my apartment and basically my life. Tell me, Paolo, what are *you* giving up in return for this cosy relationship of sex on tap and a ready incubator for your children?'

By the way his mouth was set, she could tell that his jaws were all but cemented together.

'I seem to have made a mistake.' The words hissed through his teeth. 'I thought this is what you'd want.'

Nerve connections snapped in her brain. 'You *thought* this is what I'd want!' She shook her head. 'I don't understand. What gives you the right to decide or even to think you know what's best for me? Didn't it ever occur to you that I might have an idea of what I might like myself? Who do you think you are—my father?'

He sat bolt upright. 'What are you saying?'

'He had plans for me as well. He never asked me what I wanted either.'

'I saved you from your father!'

'I thought you did—at the time. But now you're doing the exact same thing—telling me what I can and can't do. I thought I was free from having a control freak run my life—and for twelve liberated years I was. Then you had to come back.'

She gasped for air, letting him work out the rest.

Her breathing was fast and furious, her cheeks so hot that it was clear her anger had translated into more than harsh words.

He said nothing as the pulse in his temple worked overtime. Instead he glanced down at his watch and lifted himself out of his chair with a sharp exhalation of air. 'It's time we were getting back.'

Without waiting for her, he thrust some notes into the waiter's hands and strode from the restaurant.

Neither spoke on the way back to the villa, but the way he drove told her exactly how he felt. He handled the Ferrari like an extension of himself, powering confidently through the curves, eating up the bitumen with a controlled determination. The car did exactly what he wanted. No wonder he liked it.

She was glad for the silence. Their argument and the sun had left her with a niggling headache. He pulled up in the courtyard, stopping long enough to see her out of the car before disappearing abruptly into the house.

'How did you like the lake?' called Carmela from the garden, wandering over towards the car. Even in gardening clothes and with a wisp of her strong hair escaped from the clasp holding it behind, Paolo's mother looked cool and elegant.

'Just beautiful,' replied Helene, smiling as she accepted the older woman's arm in hers. 'I didn't realise how perfect it was. You're lucky to have it so close.'

'Oh, where's Paolo?' Carmela asked, looking around. 'I thought we might all have coffee together.' Then she waved the hand holding her gardening gloves. 'Of course, he will be in a hurry to get organised, no doubt. It's a shame he must leave so soon.'

'So soon?'

Carmela stopped and turned to her, frowning slightly. 'He did tell you about the New York trip? He's leaving tonight.'

'Oh, yes,' Helene said, trying to cover up the fact that he was leaving so soon was news. 'Of course.'

Helene headed for their suite to find Paolo. She had an apology to make and she wasn't looking forward to it, not after the day they'd had. She entered their bedroom, spying an open suitcase on the ancient blanket box at the end of their bed.

Paolo emerged from the walk-in wardrobe carrying shirts and a handful of silk ties. He took one look at her standing by the door before continuing directly to the suitcase, dropping in the ties and removing the hangers. His easy disregard of her was like a slap in the face.

'Why didn't you tell me you were leaving so soon?'

'Would it have mattered?'

His words sliced through her. It did matter, more than he knew. 'How long will you be gone?'

He folded the shirts loosely and stacked them in before returning to the wardrobe.

'A week, maybe two.'

Her heart squeezed tight. She didn't want him to go for a minute. She wanted to be with him. She loved curling into him at night after they'd made love and having his hands stroke her to sleep. After years of sleeping alone she had no desire to rush back to it.

'Your mother and I had a long chat.'

Her words were met with stony silence and she gulped in a breath, looking for strength. She waited for him to re-enter the room before she continued. 'She said this case you're working on is all *pro bono* work—that you and the firm receive no money. That you're providing your services free of charge.'

'That's right,' he said, shrugging. 'What of it?'

'I said some things—about you not taking on the case because you didn't need any more money. I want to apologise. I had no idea.'

He held his hands wide open after dropping a silk robe and some trunks on top of the shirts.

'But you're right. I don't need the money.'

'You're not making this any easier for me,' she accused.

'You have such a low opinion of me, why should that come as a surprise?'

'Well, I just wanted to let you know that I'm sorry.' Given the circumstances it sounded painfully inadequate. Carmela had spent the time it took to serve the coffee to fill her in on the class action his firm was fighting against a cartel of powerful pharmaceutical companies across three continents. She'd known the basic details from the reports in the papers, but she'd had no idea of the details or that without Paolo's firm's intervention the case, and with it any chance of compensation for ongoing medical costs for the child victims, would have been lost months ago.

In so many ways it echoed the work she did providing education programmes for women and children in Third World countries, work of which she was immensely proud.

'I knew you were working on a major case and yet I had no concept as to how important it was.'

One hand still arranging the things in his case, he angled his head over his shoulder and looked at her properly for the first time, one eyebrow arched speculatively. 'And if I was doing it for the money, it wouldn't be important? I'm afraid I don't understand your concept of importance, Helene. For instance, what is it that makes you believe your work is more important than having this child?'

'That's not true! I don't.'

He turned fully. 'Then why are you so determined to return to Paris and go on with your life as if this child had never been conceived?'

'I've never said that. You were the one who engineered that outcome!'

He uttered a torrent of Italian expletives, his hands palm up in the air between them. 'What was all that about earlier today, then? You made it perfectly obvious that your choice was to return to work rather than raise this child.'

'Choice? I don't remember discussing anything to do with making a choice, or even being given one. You told me what you'd decided and you expected me to fall in with your plans exactly as you've been doing ever since you reappeared in my life. So don't talk to me about what I have chosen to do—you're the least qualified person in the world to do that. You've never even bothered to consult me on the topic.'

He'd never thought of green as a hot colour, but

the way her eyes were flashing right now told him a different story. They pierced like lasers, while her cheeks betrayed her inner heat with colour, her chest by the way it rose and fell so dramatically.

He hauled in a breath as his body stirred. There was an energy about her tonight, a passion that fired his own desires. She was so beautiful, but angry like this she was magnificent. He watched the heated rise and fall of her chest and almost groaned.

He would miss those breasts. He would miss the way they responded in his mouth. He would miss the way they tasted.

He would miss all of her.

Right now he didn't want her angry. He wanted her chest to be heaving for an entirely different reason. Before he left he would have to have her.

Dredging up a laugh to break the mounting tension in the room, he put his hands on her shoulders. 'You are taking things too much to heart. My sister warned me that pregnant women are sometimes emotional. I should have remembered that today. I could have saved you both an outburst and an apology.'

'No!' She lifted her arms and broke his grip, spinning away across the room. 'Don't patronise me. This has nothing to do with me being pregnant!'

'Then tell me,' he invited soothingly, moving ever closer to her, slipping one hand around her neck. 'What is it about?'

His change of tone had caught her unawares. Her eyes seemed suddenly too big for her face, her skin now so pale it looked almost translucent, her breathing still choppy but now holding an edge, betraying an inner turmoil of a different kind.

'It's about me making my own decisions,' she said softly, her head leaning towards the warmth of his hand even though he saw the battle going on in her eyes not to.

'And I don't let you.' His other hand followed the lead of the first and he just rested his forearms on her shoulders, stroking the nape of her neck with his fingertips.

Her eyelids closed. 'No. You expect me to act like your precious Ferrari.'

'I do?'

He drew closer, his lips brushing her brow, his fingers laced through her hair.

'You do! You steer left, the car goes left. You steer right, the car goes right.'

'What can I say?' he asked, sliding his arms down her back and easing her towards him in the process. 'It's a car.'

'But I'm not. And yet you expect to steer me exactly the same way.' She gasped as his hands found their way under her ruffled skirt and slipped under the edge of her brief panties.

He covered her gasp with his mouth, softly pressing his lips over hers so that when she breathed in she would breathe his scent before he lifted his lips away.

Her hands lifted to his shoulders and she clung to him as if she would otherwise fall. Her eyes looked up at him, openly curious as her tongue found her lips. 'Your problem is you don't like it when I don't want to be driven. You can't accept that sometimes I want to be in the driver's seat. That I'm more than qualified to drive.'

He lowered his mouth to her throat while insinuating his fingers through the spring of her curls, gently opening her to his touch only to be welcomed by her slick, wet heat.

'*Dio,*' he uttered, 'I have a problem.'

'You agree?' Her voice caught as his fingers circled the sensitive flesh.

'I have never known anyone who makes me feel so inadequate. I have no control where you are concerned. Wanting you is *driving* me crazy.'

Her flesh was growing moister, her words breathier. 'You know that's not what I meant.'

'But it is true. And I am leaving it up to you.' Slowly, reluctantly, he withdrew his hand and lifted her two hands away from his shoulders. Her eyes looked dazed and she blinked, unsteady with his sudden loss of support. 'What do you want? I am giving you the choice whether or not we make love now. You decide.'

Already her body was humming from his sensual touch, her breathing shallow in anticipation of that place where only he could take her. Already she could feel her body preparing itself for sex, nerve endings alive and receptive. So what kind of choice was he giving her? No choice at all.

But he thought he had her. He thought she was so far gone she was his for the taking. Desire reached out from his dark, confident eyes, coiling around her as he waited. But it wasn't the kind of choice she needed, even if it took her every shred of self-control she had.

She let him stand there, watching her, and then slowly, sensually she slid her hands until they crossed over at the hem of her top as if she were going to peel it off. His eyes followed every tiny movement so that she recognised the very moment his pupils dilated as he took the gesture for compliance, noticed his rapid intake of air and the twitch of the muscle in his jaw as he silently urged her on. She read hunger in his eyes, she could taste his anticipation.

'Actually,' she said, rearranging her hands into an innocent clasp in front of her, 'given that you're going to leave so soon, it's probably not a good idea to interrupt your packing.'

His nostrils flared, his eyes widened with disbelief on reflex. 'You're saying no?'

It was her turn to raise one eyebrow at him. 'Unless you really want to?'

They never made it to the bed, not the first time at least. He took her there, passionately, desperately, right where she was, her legs drawn up tightly around him, and only when the last shuddering waves rocked through her and her legs slid down to find support did they collapse together onto the bed so that he could make love to her all over again.

It was some time before they moved. 'I have to leave now,' he whispered in her ear, kissing her lightly. She must have dozed while he'd showered and changed. 'My car will be here shortly.'

Heaviness filled her muscles and the shadow of a headache from her day at the lake had built to something more. Even the afterglow she was used to feeling low down after orgasm had staled into something more like an insistent ache. A sudden moment of panic gripped her and she sat up. 'I don't want you to go.'

'I have to go,' he said. 'But what we talked about at lunch—' He dipped his head in a nod. 'You were right. I didn't ever ask you what you wanted. But I know we can build a family around this child.' He kissed her again lightly on the lips, picked up his jacket and suitcase and headed for the door.

Her heart hammered loud in her chest. Should she tell him now before he went away? Tell him the truth—tell him that she loved him and she would stay with him for ever, on whatever terms? Her lips fought to frame the words.

'Paolo.' Even as her teeth dragged over her bottom lip she knew that she couldn't. He couldn't love her— not if he was leaving her so suddenly this way. The last thing he'd want to hear right now was her telling him that she loved him. He'd never believe her now.

But she couldn't let him go entirely without him giving her something, a kernel of hope, something for her to hold onto. 'I need to ask something before you go.'

'What?'

'I know this child is very important to you and I understand that. It's very important to me too. But I need to know...' She hesitated in the silence while he waited. 'I need to know if I'm important to you too.'

His eyes narrowed immediately, creasing at the sides as if the question was all too easy. 'After what we just shared you have to ask? But of course you're important to me. Apart from the sex, you're carrying my child.'

The pain woke her from a fitful sleep. Sharp spasms racked her insides, the cramps acute, and for a few minutes she desperately feared the worst. But then the sickness rose in her throat and it was almost with relief that she staggered to the bathroom. It *had* to be food poisoning, even though she knew she'd barely touched her lunch and hadn't felt like dinner.

It just had to be.

CHAPTER TWELVE

THE cab topped the small rise and the outline of New York City appeared on the skyline before them. Yet today Paolo felt none of the excitement he usually did *en route* from the airport, no anticipation of the battle to come, none of his usual hunger to win.

Instead his thoughts centred squarely on home. Leaving had been one of the hardest things he'd done in a long time and that in itself was a surprise. But the fact he'd been unable to shift his thoughts and focus on the brief in front of him all throughout the long flight was even more unsettling.

But it was hardly home he was thinking about—it was Helene. He'd never been so wholly distracted by thoughts of anyone before. Even the guilt following Sapphy's sudden marriage to Sheikh Khaled Al-Ateeq, both the guilt that he hadn't been honest enough with her to prevent her from going to Jebbai in the first place and guilt that his inability to do so had resulted in a marriage borne out of revenge, didn't come close to what he was feeling now.

It was Helene and her compassion one night in Paris that had got him through that time and it was Helene and the look on her face just before he'd walked out of their room that haunted him now. She'd looked so fragile, so sad. Why should she be sad?

She'd asked him what she meant to him and he'd told her exactly how important she was to him. Yet

157

her face had fallen, her eyes had grown more crystalline. Had she been expecting something different? Something more?

A sudden memory collided into his thoughts like an express train. There was only one thing more.

'What about love?' she'd asked him at lunch, and he'd answered her honestly. But to then ask him whether or not she was important to him—was that what she'd been leading up to? Had she wanted him to say that he loved her?

It made no sense. She was the one who wanted out of their relationship, after all. She was the one who wanted to get back to Paris and resume her precious career as soon as possible, even sooner if he would let her run a home office from the villa. She was the one who kept denying him at every turn. Those things were hardly the actions of someone in love.

No, he decided, their relationship was purely physical. They shared great sex and a growing baby. That should be enough for anyone.

Traffic was heavy and it was taking for ever to get to his hotel, so he requested the taxi driver to drop him off near the office. He'd got nothing done on the plane and he would probably end up wasting everyone's time because of it, but at least there he might be able to focus on the case.

By the time he'd checked into the hotel he'd been awake for more hours than he cared to think about, but at least finally he'd made some progress. Tomorrow he could start to assemble the team.

'Oh, and there's a message for you, sir.' The concierge handed him his room card in a small folder together with an envelope.

His mind in autopilot during the formalities, Paolo scooped them both up in one hand and headed for the lifts. Only after he'd discarded his bag and jacket and poured himself a slug of scotch did he notice the envelope on the credenza where he'd tossed it upon entering the room. He tore it open and froze. The message from his mother was chillingly brief.

'Urgent. Call home immediately.'

Helene!

It was insane—in his mind he recognised the emergency could involve any one of his family or anything and yet in his heart he knew instinctively that it had to be Helene and that she was in danger.

Panic gripped him as he battled with the phone for an international connection. He couldn't bear it if she was hurt—or worse. Nothing must happen to her. She was part of him now, a part he never intended to lose.

He'd misdialled the number for the second time when it hit him. He hadn't given a thought to their child—Helene had been his first and only concern. The truth slammed his heart against his chest wall as the one thing he'd thought not possible screamed out its truth.

He loved her.

Fear lurched inside him. The truth was staggering in itself, but it was the implications that made him reel, made him throw his hand to his forehead as the ramifications of his discovery hit home.

He'd told Helene that all she meant to him was nothing more than good sex and as the mother of his child. He'd as good as told her that that was all there could ever be. And he'd thought he was doing the right thing—but when he recalled her eyes, so lost and hurting as he'd turned and walked away...

Dio! He was half a world away and he loved her and she didn't know and if anything happened to her...

Frantically he stabbed at the buttons of the phone and after an interminable wait for a connection he made it through at last. The housekeeper answered on the third ring despite it being something like five a.m. her time. She promptly burst into tears amidst a torrent of impassioned words, but in a few short seconds his worst fears were realised.

His blood turned to ice.

Helene was in hospital.

And she'd lost the baby.

She was empty inside, empty of the new life she'd nurtured in her body these past seventeen weeks, empty of her hopes and dreams for the future—a future that now stretched out as bleak and barren as she felt within.

No baby. No precious child to hold in her arms, no tiny fingers to cling to her own, no sweet features to soothe into sleep.

She couldn't stay at the villa. She'd checked herself out of hospital saying she'd be better off in her own bed, but there was no reason to stay. There was no point pretending any more.

She'd lost his child.

He didn't want her love.

There was nothing she could offer Paolo now.

Another wave of grief washed over her, filling the yawning spaces inside with pain and hurt.

She'd wanted this child so much! Whatever custodial or living arrangements Paolo and she had eventually settled upon wouldn't have mattered in the end. This would have been her child and she would have loved it and nurtured it regardless. She would have showered upon it all the love that she had been denied her entire life. Whatever else might have happened, her baby would always have had a mother.

But now there was no chance to be that mother.

Now she had nothing.

No baby, no future, no hope that Paolo would want her.

She clasped her hands protectively low over her stomach—she couldn't stop herself—even though she knew there was no point and that it was too late. There was no child any more.

It was too hard to accept. Being told she was pregnant had been a struggle to accept, certainly, but the knowledge that she was no longer with child was any number of times more impossible to come to terms with. Even when she'd felt that one godawful paroxysm that had left her feeling as if it had torn her apart inside, she'd been in denial. It hadn't been until the warm swell of moisture and the trickle down her thigh that she'd known there was no point kidding herself any more.

She sucked in a breath of air as she did a mental stocktake of what she'd need. The doctors and Carmela had ordered her to stay in bed and rest, but she was sick of the inactivity, sick of thinking endlessly about what might have gone wrong. Thinking about what she must have done wrong.

So instead, she moved about the room, packing only what she could carry in a small overnight bag. She'd get a taxi to pick her up. They could send the rest of her gear on, but she had to leave now, before he arrived.

Because there was no way she could face him.

She'd lost him his child and there was no way he would ever forgive her. And she couldn't face another scene, not now. Besides which, there was no point.

There was no reason now to continue their farce of a marriage, no tie to bind them together and certainly no reason to imagine he'd want to stand by his offer of making a family together. She'd let him down, and the sooner she removed herself from his life, the sooner he could find himself a real wife. The sooner he could find someone he loved.

She picked up a few items from her dressing table, her eyes falling on the crystal heart paperweight that he'd bought her in New York. She picked it up, feeling its cool weight in her hands. Her own heart squeezed tight when she remembered the day he'd bought it. He'd been so controlling, insisting on spending a fortune on rings when the last thing she felt like was a bride, and then he'd surprised her completely by gifting her the heart. And she'd thought— she'd hoped—that maybe they could make this work. But it would never work. There was too much history between them, too little love.

At long last he could get on with lodging the paperwork they'd both signed and made ready for their divorce months ago. At last he'd be free of her. The inconvenience was over, the lies and the deceit needed no longer.

Reluctantly she replaced the paperweight on the table, tracing her fingers around its sculpted sides. She didn't want any tender reminders of this time that might cause her to regret what she was doing. She *was* doing the right thing. She had no choice. Now that she was no longer bearing his child he didn't need her any more. He wouldn't want her to stay.

And she had to get out before he asked her to leave.

She removed her rings, the plain white-gold wedding band and the stunning three-diamond engagement ring he'd insisted she have. The skin underneath looked pale after the Italian sunshine and she rubbed absently at the mark as if she could somehow eradicate the past few months by removing all trace of it. Then she put the rings down alongside the heart. Whatever they thought of her after her departure, it wasn't going to be that she was a bloodsucking witch, out for anything she could get.

A sob lodged in her throat when she thought of what she was about to do, leaving Carmela without a word. It wasn't right, but she knew that if she tried to say goodbye the older woman would make her stay and face Paolo and there was no way she could cope with that. Carmela didn't understand because she didn't know the truth, and this was hardly the time to tell her.

Her minimalist packing completed, she propped up a letter she'd written for Paolo alongside the rings and the heart before taking one more look around the room where she'd been so happy with Paolo, in bed at least. She had some good memories—great memories—to take away with her. She'd seen both tenderness and passion, felt his gentle hands and his surging power, tasted his liquid mouth and his velvet heat.

But it was time to order her taxi and leave. She picked up the telephone at exactly the same time it started to ring.

She froze. She'd picked up on an incoming call. What if it was Paolo calling? What would she say?

Her heart hammering, she put the receiver up to her ear, but it was a woman's voice that met her silence—her Italian fluent yet with a trace of an accent. She recognised Paolo's name and blinked.

'I'm sorry,' she said in English, without the energy to try to respond in her faltering Italian. 'I'm afraid Paolo is unavailable just at the moment. Can I help you?'

Her earlier silence was now mirrored at the other end.

'Is that…Helene?'

She couldn't speak. Why would this stranger be calling Paolo on his unlisted family home number, for a start, let alone know about her? There was only one person this could be…

'Who's calling, please?' she managed to get out, doing her best to sound calm and professional even while her fingers clawed white-knuckled on the receiver and her pulse thrummed loud in her ears.

'It's Sapphire Clem— I mean…' She laughed a little as if a little nervous, a little uncertain. 'I mean— just Sapphy. I'm an old friend of Paolo's and I need to talk to him.'

Oh, God. Helene closed her eyes, her free arm

steadying her against the table, wishing she had already left.

Suddenly the accent made sense. It belonged to Sapphire Clemenger, the fashion designer he would have married if not for the small complication that he'd already been married to Helene, and the woman Paolo loved.

But how did Sapphire know about Helene?

And why was she calling Paolo now?

Unless she needed help to escape from Khaled? And who else would she call but the man she should have been with?

New resolve gripped her. This was Helene's chance to make up for the mess she'd created over twelve years ago. Now she could finally put things to right between Paolo and Sapphire. They deserved every chance to be together. They deserved to be happy.

'I'm sorry,' she said at last. 'Paolo won't be home until later, so if you'd like to call again?'

'I won't have a chance,' Sapphire responded. 'I'm about to board my flight to Milan. But it's great to hear that he'll be there. Please let him know I'm on my way.'

Helene put the receiver down, resting both hands on the phone as she took some welcome deep breaths. It was good that Sapphire was coming. It was right. A tear rolled down her cheek. Even though her own heart was broken, there was no need for Paolo to go without happiness. After all he'd done for her, the years he'd wasted on her behalf, he deserved his chance to love.

She picked up the receiver again, ordered a taxi in

her stammering Italian and, after seizing a stack of tissues to mop up her leaking eyes, quietly exited the house to wait.

She was gone. For the second time she'd left him, leaving only a few written lines in her wake. Guilt that he should have been here with her, guilt that somehow he was responsible for what had happened by his persistent lovemaking—all his guilt evaporated as his eyes slid over the contents of the brief note yet again.

Paolo,
I couldn't stay after what's happened. I'm so sorry about the baby. I know what having a child meant to you, but maybe this way is for the best.
Now there is no need to pretend any longer.
Thank you so much for rescuing me so long ago and for standing by me all these years. I'm sorry that I couldn't repay you in a better way—you deserve much more.
Goodbye,
Helene

Paolo threw back his head and roared, his cry a rough animal mix of anguish, despair and heated fury. How dared she say that this was for the best?

His child was dead! How could such a tragedy ever be for the best?

It might be for her. She'd wanted out of their arrangement as soon as she could, wanting out of any chance of a life with him, wanting to return to her neat life and her perfect career. A miscarriage must have suited her perfectly.

And he'd imagined she loved him! He'd even convinced himself that he loved her. He must have been insane.

She couldn't wait to get out of here. She couldn't wait to get away from him.

So much for love.

CHAPTER THIRTEEN

SHE'D been kidding herself. Helene tossed the last of her laundry into the machine and followed it with an unusually reckless dose of powder. She'd thought when she'd left the villa that she was leaving behind all trace of Paolo and what had happened between them, but even her apartment was full of memories.

Nowhere provided the sanctuary she needed. His presence was right through the place—from the reception room where he'd studied the items on her mantelpiece with such apparent fascination before their torrid lovemaking, to the bedroom where even now she imagined she could smell his scent on the sheets alongside her.

Everywhere held memories of him and every part of her empty life threw into sharp relief exactly how much she'd lost.

Everything.

But the very worst part of it all was knowing that she'd made the right decision. It was two weeks since she'd returned from Milan and there'd been no word from him, no effort to get in touch. She hadn't expected him to follow her, yet the fact that he hadn't made the slightest attempt to contact her simply confirmed the correctness of her actions. She'd done the right thing for both of them by leaving.

If only she felt better about it. It was one thing to want Paolo to be happy, but another thing entirely to know that he had so easily let her go. It stung. Though what had she expected? She'd just about set him up with his former lover.

She punched at the washing-machine buttons with much more force than strictly necessary before swiping from her face the strands of hair that had worked loose from her pony-tail. There was no point thinking about what might have happened between Paolo and Sapphire after she'd left. No point at all torturing herself and imagining them together. She just had to get over it.

Noises from outside her door jagged into her thoughts, jerking her head around—voices on the stairs, on the landing outside, then the sound of the neighbour's door closing before the empty resumption of quiet—and she sighed. How long would it be before she didn't jump every time she heard a footfall on the stairs, or freeze when the telephone rang? How long would it take before she felt normal again?

Another door banged shut and someone tapped on her door. She tried to extinguish the spark of hope that flickered into life as she walked towards the door, telling herself it was no doubt Eugene back from shopping with a slice of Brie or a croissant for her. But the spark raged into a firestorm when she looked through the peep-hole and saw who was standing on the other side.

Paolo.

A tidal wave of conflicting emotions crashed over her, a mess of rippling sensations assailing her senses, all conspiring to take her breath away. She clutched her hands to her chest and felt her panicked heartbeat racing beneath as she fought for air.

He was here. And just like the first time he'd appeared on her doorstep his dark eyes looked wild, his face strained and tense. Would his message this time be the same? Was that why he'd come, to deliver in person the final blow to their marriage? Was he taking the opportunity to put into words what his two weeks of failing to contact her had made plain?

She pulled open the door and reminded herself to breathe.

For a second it was almost tenderness she thought she saw in his eyes, but then he blinked and they narrowed and any tenderness slid straight off their glinting, rock-hard surface. 'You've got some explaining to do,' he said as he pushed past her into the apartment.

There was little she could do but follow him, her skin tingling where he'd brushed by, her senses reeling in the wake of his familiar scent, her late-night dreams and memories inadequate preparation for the sheer physical impact of the man.

'Why did you leave?' he demanded, his hands on his hips.

He wasn't wasting any time on pleasantries. He hadn't even bothered to sit down before he'd turned and fired the question off like a salvo. So that was how it was going to be. She pulled her loosened hair back tightly behind her ears and crossed her arms.

'I couldn't stay.'

'You mean you couldn't wait to get away.'

'It wasn't like that—'

'No? So you're not already back at work, then?'

She dropped her eyes and looked away. The doctor had pronounced her fit and she'd started back two days ago. It wasn't that she was desperate to get back, despite what Paolo thought—it had just seemed a much healthier option than moping around the apartment feeling sorry for herself.

'You couldn't wait to go back to your precious job.' He spat the words out like bullets.

'And what was I supposed to do?' she retaliated, throwing her arms out wide. 'Hang around and wait for you to arrive so you could push me around again? No, thanks, I've had enough of being pushed around for one lifetime.'

'You were supposed to be resting at the villa, not running away.'

'Who said I was running?' She hadn't been running. It had been more like a tactical withdrawal. She'd got herself out of his life before he'd thrown her out.

'You've been running all your life. Running away from your father, running away without a word the night we spent together here in this very apartment. And you're still running. You stole away from the villa like a thief.'

'And who wouldn't leave in the circumstances?'

'Any normal person! You'd just lost a baby—remember? Or were you so keen to get back to work that a mere miscarriage was too insignificant a detail to register with you?'

The cold shock of his words came with an acid burn.

'How *dare* you say that? How could I forget? I was the one who was there. It was me who felt the pain. It was me who felt my baby tearing itself free from my womb—'

Her voice cracked on the last word and she spun around, battling to regain some sort of control after her impassioned outburst.

But she didn't have a chance before his hands were on her shoulders. 'I'm sorry,' he said, turning her around to face him. 'I didn't mean that. I didn't come here today to upset you.'

'Then don't you ever say that losing our baby didn't mean anything to me. You have no idea how much I wanted that child, how much I wanted it all to turn out perfectly.' Her lip quivered. 'But it didn't. It all went wrong. I lost my baby.'

He pulled her into his arms as the bubble in her throat became a sob, opening the floodgates to her grief. 'Our baby,' he said. '*We* lost *our* baby.'

He held her tight as she cried, really cried. For two weeks she'd held herself together, defying the tears, refusing to dwell on her loss, but there was no stopping them now.

'I'm sorry,' he said, stroking her head. 'I should have been there with you.'

She sniffed, lifting her head away at last and wiping the liquid tracks of tears from her face. 'It doesn't matter now. There's nothing you could have done.'

'I should never have left you,' he insisted. 'It must have been terrifying. My mother said you were in a lot of pain.'

Reluctantly she thought back to that awful night. There had been pain, and plenty of it, and yet it wasn't the pain that was foremost in her memories of that time. 'The worst pain,' she said softly, 'was knowing there was nothing I could do. The worst pain was knowing there was no hope for our child—no chance for it at all.'

He pulled her back in close and wrapped her securely in his arms again. She met his broad chest and inhaled deeply, revelling in the feel of the muscled wall of his chest against her cheek and the musky tones of his masculine scent. She'd missed him so much and yet he hadn't bothered to follow her here until now. If he'd really wanted to be with her, to console her and share in her grief, he'd had plenty of time before now.

She eased herself out of his arms, needing to show him how strong she was, that she could cope, so that when he left her again to go back to Sapphire he would never suspect the truth. He would never know that she loved him.

'I'm sorry,' she said with a shrug, recognising the pain in his eyes because it so closely matched her own. He'd lost his child and he looked just as confused, just as bereft. 'I don't even know why it happened.'

'I made love to you before I left,' he said. 'Could I have hurt you? Was I to blame?'

His features looked so anguished that for a moment she wanted to take his face in her hands and kiss his torment away. He wasn't blaming her! It was the last thing she'd expected. She smiled a little and shook her head.

'Not a chance. The doctors said that sometimes these things just happen. They assured me that it's nothing to do with anything either of us did.'

'There must be a reason.'

She sighed, rubbing her hands together for the sake

of doing something. 'I've been thinking about that. Maybe our baby knew that things weren't right between us. Maybe somehow it didn't want to be born to people that weren't entirely happy about having it.'

'I wanted this child!'

She held up a hand to stop him. 'And you don't think I did? Of course I wanted it! But neither of us was particularly happy about the circumstances of its conception. Neither of us was happy about being forced together the way we were. We both wanted this child, certainly, but maybe—and it probably sounds crazy—but maybe, the baby just didn't want us.'

Her teeth sank down on her bottom lip and pressed tight, hoping the pain would take away another.

'That is crazy.'

'I know, but have you got a better theory? Who would want to be born into a family with so much heartache, into a relationship built on deception? You could hardly blame a child for not wanting to get tangled up in our mess.'

He shook his head, making sweeping arcs of denial with his arms as he strode around the room. She watched his progress, feeling his pain, understanding his anguish. Just as on the night he'd turned up on her doorstep four months ago, he seemed suddenly uncertain of his place in life, his natural arrogance tempered by his innate humanity. She could see the battle for understanding going on behind his weary eyes. She could feel his internal struggle.

But how could you understand something that made no sense? How could you unravel a fathomless mystery?

After a time he stopped pacing and reached a hand into the pocket of his jacket.

'I had your belongings packed, but I wanted to bring you something.' For a moment she thought he must mean her rings. He held out his hand, palm down, and she placed her hand under his, expecting something small, and so totally unprepared for the weight when he dropped the object into her hands that she almost let it spill out of her hands onto the carpet. She pulled it in close and looked down at it, her fingers curling around the edges as she studied its ruby depths.

'Why did you leave it behind?' he asked.

'I couldn't bear to take it,' she replied honestly, two fat tears rolling silently down her cheeks as she remembered the scan, the transparent flesh, the tiny beating heart. 'I was too raw and it reminded me of something much, much too special.'

He nodded, coming closer to look at it in her hands. 'The first time I saw it in the display cabinet, it made me think of the scan—'

She looked up at him, blinking away the moisture in her eyes only to notice the sheen in his. He'd seen their baby's heart in the simple paperweight too?

'Why are you here?' she asked hesitantly. She didn't know why she should feel hope, except that this wasn't turning out to be the blamefest she'd expected from Paolo's visit. 'You didn't come just to bring me this.'

'No.' He sucked in a burst of air and expelled it in a rush. 'I didn't.'

She waited, her hands squeezing the crystal heart as if it might lend her some of its cool, hard strength.

'I've lodged the papers to finalise our divorce.'

CHAPTER FOURTEEN

THE oxygen was sucked from the room, the ticking clock the only sound in the vacuum of Helene's world.

'Ah. I see.' How not to sound disappointed when the bottom was dropping out of her world? She'd known this was going to happen, had suspected the wheels were already well and truly in motion. But still, Paolo's words were final confirmation that he was happy to let her go, that, now the child they'd both had a part in making was lost, he had no further need for her.

She sat down on her settee, feigning interest in placing the crystal heart down on the coffee-table in just the right position. 'Of course, I expected as much. I know it's taken much longer than what we ever anticipated.' She tried to laugh, but the sound came out broken and flat. 'Who would ever have imagined our rushed marriage would have lasted so long? At last now you can finally be free.'

A muscle twitched in his jaw. 'If everything goes to plan, I'm not planning on being free for long.'

Prickly fingers skittered down her spine before grabbing hold of her heart and squeezing it tightly. Surely not already? 'I'm afraid I'm not with you.'

'I'm planning to get married again.'

What was left of her heart dropped to her feet. There was only one person he could be marrying. It

176

didn't matter that this was the very thing she'd expected when she'd left, that this was how she'd envisaged their futures working out. Now it was real, it was happening and it hurt so very badly.

'I understand.' The words squeezed out through her teeth. 'How is Sapphire?'

His coal-black lashes tangled together in a blink that seemed to last an eternity. Then they opened to a twitch in his jaw. 'That was you she spoke to when she called the villa? We suspected it must be, but we had no idea when you'd left.'

She nodded. 'I'm sorry, she said to leave you a note. I forgot...'

He considered her response for only a moment. 'It's of no consequence. She's well, as it happens. Better than well. In fact, I've never seen her looking so happy.'

Every word was like a spike to her soul. Every word sealed her fate a little more securely. Paolo would divorce her and marry Sapphy and once more she would be alone.

'I'm so glad,' she lied, determined to put on a brave face. 'You both deserve to be happy after all that's happened. I feel so responsible for the whole mess—you were so right—if it hadn't been for me running from my father and that forced marriage to Khaled, none of this would have happened. So it's right that you two have been able to salvage something from the wreckage. It's good that you can finally be together.'

'Together?' His brows drew close as he frowned. 'What makes you say that?'

'Well, you and Sapphire. I thought that—that you and she…now that you were free…'

'You thought I was planning on marrying Sapphy?'

'Aren't you?'

'She's married already, and she's staying married.'

'But that's to Khaled!'

'I know, it's hard to believe. But like I said, she's the happiest I've ever seen her. She's in love with him, I have no doubt of that.'

'And what about him?'

He nodded. 'I met Khaled. Sapphire brought him with her. She didn't say anything about her plans during her call because she thought I'd refuse to see him.'

Helene shivered, wrapping her arms around herself. It was just as well she'd left the villa. There was no way she could have handled seeing Khaled again, knowing what she'd done all those years ago. Her simple teenage act of defiance had spawned more than a decade of hatred and retribution. Coming on the heels of her miscarriage, even being in the same house with him would have been unbearable.

And yet it must have been almost as difficult for Paolo, if not more so, given that he had lost the woman he loved to him.

'But you saw him?' she asked, her curiosity about the man she had snubbed so long ago intensely aroused, despite the dark place he'd always occupied in her mind. 'I couldn't,' she said with a shiver. 'To hate someone for so long just because he married the woman promised to you first—I don't think I could handle meeting him.'

'I thought the same thing at first. But I finally discovered that there was more to his desire for revenge against me than having lost you. I discovered he held me responsible for the sudden death of his parents and that's what really drove him to do what he did.'

'But that's crazy. Why would he possibly believe you had anything to do with his parents?'

'They died in an avalanche in the Alps. It never occurred to me that it had happened the same day he was supposed to marry you.'

'Oh, my God!' The full ramifications of what he was explaining sank in. 'So they should have been in London attending the wedding and not in the Alps at all? And he held you responsible for that because you married me instead?'

'So it would seem. I'd stolen you away and the wedding plans were aborted. His parents left for the Alps to get over their disappointment. They were killed outright by the avalanche, along with their two companions.'

'How horrible,' she said on a shudder, finally starting to understand what might possibly drive a man to hate so much. 'But he came to Milan with Sapphire? What's changed that he would want to meet with you, after all that's happened?'

'Sapphy's changed him, for a start. It seems that he would never have made any attempt at reconciliation if not for her influence. He really does love her. But that's not all. It seem recent events in Jebbai have thrown doubt on the circumstances of the tragedy. There's a chance the avalanche wasn't an accident at all, that it was triggered by one or both of the companions.'

'Khaled's parents were assassinated?'

'They now suspect that may be true. The companions' daughter was involved in an attempt on Khaled's life recently. They thought initially it was just in retribution for the death of her parents in the avalanche, but now it seems the entire family has been involved in actions against the Sheikhdom all along—a grudge going back generations.'

'So Khaled now knows that you weren't responsible for his parents' deaths.'

He nodded. 'But that's not all. They believe the original plan was to carry out their grisly task at the wedding.' He paused. 'Your wedding with Khaled.'

Her blood turned to ice as she thought about the long guest list her mother had organised and the no doubt packed church. 'It could have been all of us there that day.' She looked up at him as the truth rammed home. 'You saved our lives. All our lives that day—including Khaled's.'

'Ironic, isn't it?' he said with a wry laugh. 'And yet he'd blamed me for stealing his bride and destroying the lives of his parents. When if we hadn't married all those years ago...' His words trailed off. 'Well, we did marry.'

It was impossible to absorb it all. Too much was happening. Too much was changing. She stood up and wandered over to the long window, pulling aside the soft muslin curtain and gazing out over the narrow street outside, the apartment buildings jammed together with their quaint metal balconies, the picturebook roof-line jutting into the summer sky, the people walking down the street. It all looked so perfectly normal. It all looked so perfectly ordinary. And yet she knew things could never be normal or ordinary again. The components of her world had shifted like vast plates moving roughly over each other, altering the connections and changing the relationships for ever.

She turned away from the window, looking back at him. 'I always thought of you as saving me from a fate worse than death, but I never realised how literally true that was. You saved me from more than a forced marriage I never wanted. You actually saved my life by marrying me.'

He held his hands palm up. 'None of it is proven. We can't be sure.'

'I'm sure,' she insisted. 'But I just don't know how I ever am ever going to repay you.'

'I didn't tell you all that so that you would feel you had to repay me. I told you so that you would understand Khaled and see that he is no longer a threat to your happiness.'

She smiled as she moved closer, reaching one tentative hand up to his cheek. 'You have done more for me than any person on this earth. You stepped in when I most needed a friend, when I had lost my family and I was alone and frightened. And you lived with the promise of Khaled's revenge for years because of it.

'I know there's nothing I can offer in return, I know there's no reason for you to have anything to do with me in the future, but if you ever need anything, anything, then please let me know.'

He took her hand in his, holding it against his cheek. 'There is one thing you can do for me,' he said, his voice gravelly and low, his eyes so intense they seemed to pierce into her soul.

'Marry me,' he said. 'Become my wife. Be part of my life for ever.'

She blinked her eyes, but the dream didn't disappear—Paolo was still there and the magic was still fizzing in her veins.

'You can't be serious,' she said. 'We are—*were*—married. You've just lodged the papers for our divorce.'

'No. We had a certificate of marriage, that's all. We were never really married, not properly. I lodged those divorce papers because that marriage never really existed. And I should have lodged them four months ago when you signed them but I couldn't bring myself to do it. I couldn't take that last step to sever the ties we'd created back then, especially after that night together with you.'

'You told me you didn't have time to lodge them.'

'I know. Because I could hardly tell you the truth. That night we shared was special for me. I wasn't prepared to let you go so easily after that. I used the fact we were still married to force you into coming back to Milan, even though it was clear you wanted to be rid of me.'

'What do you mean—it was clear?'

'You signed those papers and left them where I couldn't miss them. They could have waited. There was no rush.'

'Oh, Paolo! But when you turned up looking so desperate, I thought that's exactly what you wanted—to be free of me for ever. I'd already taken up enough of your life.'

He took her hands and kissed them. 'It will never be enough,' he said. 'But I want the chance to start again with you, Helene. I want a real marriage. And this is the hardest thing of all for me, but this time I won't tell you what to do and I won't force you into anything. This time it's your choice. This time you get to decide.'

There was no way she couldn't smile. There was no way her smile wouldn't light up a darkened room, she felt so happy. 'I can't believe this is happening. I thought you were angry with me. When you didn't contact me here I thought you never wanted to see me again—'

He took her hands in his. 'I'm so sorry I let you think that. When I discovered you'd gone I went crazy. I was angry that our child was gone—so damned angry that you'd left that I couldn't think straight. My mother, my sister, even Sapphy—they all urged me to go after you immediately, but I thought I could forget you.'

He took a deep breath before continuing. 'Except as the days went by I realised what made me the angriest—it was because I'd lost you without ever telling you how much you meant to me. It was because if I didn't go after you I'd never get the chance to tell you, and, no matter what your reaction, I had to try.'

She swallowed, terrified that he wasn't going to say what she so wanted to hear.

'I'd fallen in love with you, Helene. I tried to suppress it; I tried to bury it under my anger and grief, I tried to think that you meant only sex and a child to me, but the truth wouldn't be denied. And I know that you have plenty of reasons to say no, but I'm asking you—begging you to say yes. Please marry me. Give us the chance to start again. Because there's no way I can live without you. I love you.'

He loved her? Elation pumped through her veins. It hardly seemed possible—she was hearing the words she'd longed to hear from the man she had loved for what seemed like for ever. And he was asking her to marry him. *Really* marry him.

'Yes,' she said, watching her own delight mirrored as his face lit up at her simple word. 'Yes, I will marry you. Yes, I love you. Yes! Yes! Yes!'

Laughing, she threw her arms around his neck as he swept her up, whirling her around in his arms as his lips met hers in a hungry kiss that spoke of their weeks of separation and their commitment to a long future together.

Breathless, he pulled his head away at last. 'You love me? You said you loved me.'

'You crazy man,' she said. 'I was in love with you the first time I married you. And this time I love you even more.'

'I had no idea,' he said, his eyes wide, searching her face.

'Wait,' she said as inspiration hit. 'I'll be right back.' She left him there behind her, a look of wonderment on his face, while she disappeared into her room. In thirty seconds she was back.

'I've always loved you, Paolo,' she said, taking his hand and sliding the ring on. 'This is a token of my love. All those years of separation I tried to forget you, but it didn't happen. I could get on with my life, but I couldn't get you out of my heart.'

His light frown turned to amazement when he recognised his old signet ring. 'You've had this all that time?'

'All that time.' She smiled. 'I've treasured it and now I want you to have it and wear it as a sign of how far we've come, as confirmation of my undying love for you.'

He shook his head as if it was all too much to take in, then his features edged into a frown.

'What is it?' she asked.

He smiled. 'Something Sapphy said to me when she came to the villa. She said that all the time she was with me she sensed there was always a part of me that would never be hers, that it always seemed as if there was something holding me back.'

'But you couldn't commit to her. Not when you were already married.'

'No,' he said, 'it was more than that and Sapphy recognised it and I've only just realised that what she said was right. Because a piece of paper would never have been enough to stop me giving my heart and soul to her if it had been free to give. It would never have stopped me loving her. But it did. Because someone already had my heart.' He touched his index finger to the tip of her nose. 'You.'

He'd loved her all that time? It was more than a dream. It was a fantasy come to life and she never wanted it to end.

'Are you telling me that you loved me all those years ago?'

'I think I must have. I didn't want Khaled to have you; I know that. Why would I have married you if I didn't love you?'

'But we never... I mean, you wouldn't—'

'I must have been mad. But I didn't want to take advantage of you that night. I didn't want you to think I would expect sex for payment for what I'd done when I wasn't entirely sure of my motives.'

'You have to be kidding me. You loved me all that time and you've only just realised it now?'

'Guilty,' he said, drawing her close to him again, nuzzling the skin below her ear.

'Then I'd say we have a few years of loving to make up for.'

He pulled back and looked at her, his mouth curved up into a sexy smile, his eyes glinting with resolve, and one look at his lips told her he was going to kiss her, and that he was going to be kissing her for a long, long time to come.

Then his mouth dipped down to hers, his lips a mere breath away. 'So when do we start?'

Look forward to all these ⋆ ⋆ wonderful books this ⋆ Christmas ⋆

All I want for **Christmas**

BETTY NEELS
MARGARET WAY
JESSICA STEELE

Precious Gifts

Together for **Christmas**

Lynnette Kent & Sherryl Woods

Jennie Cresswell Kate Hoffmann
Tara Taylor Quinn

The **CHRISTMAS VISIT**

Margaret Moore
Gail Ranstrom
Terri Brisbin

SILHOUETTE
SNOWY NIGHTS

MILLS & BOON®
Live the emotion

Modern
romance™

THE DISOBEDIENT VIRGIN by Sandra Marton

Catarina Mendes has been dictated to all her life. Now, with her twenty-first birthday, comes freedom – but it's freedom at a price. Jake Ramirez has become her guardian. He must find a man for her to marry. But Jake is so overwhelmed by her beauty that he is tempted to keep Cat for himself...

A SCANDALOUS MARRIAGE by Miranda Lee

Sydney entrepreneur Mike Stone has a month to get married – or he'll lose a business deal worth billions. Natalie Fairlane, owner of the *Wives Wanted* introduction agency, is appalled by his proposition! But the exorbitant fee Mike is offering for a temporary wife is *very* tempting...!

SLEEPING WITH A STRANGER by Anne Mather

Helen Shaw's holiday on the island of Santos should be relaxing. But then she sees Greek tycoon Milos Stephanides. Years ago they had an affair – until, discovering he was untruthful, Helen left him. Now she has something to hide from Milos...

AT THE ITALIAN'S COMMAND by Cathy Williams

Millionaire businessman Rafael Loro is used to beautiful women who agree to his every whim – until he employs dowdy but determined Sophie Frey! Sophie drives him crazy! But once he succeeds in bedding her, his thoughts of seduction turn into a need to possess her...

On sale 4th November 2005

Available at most branches of WHSmith, Tesco, ASDA, Borders, Eason, Sainsbury's and most bookshops

Visit www.millsandboon.co.uk

MILLS & BOON®

1005/01b

Live the emotion

Modern
romance™

PRINCE'S PLEASURE by Carole Mortimer

Reporter Tyler Harwood is ecstatic when she gets the chance to interview handsome Hollywood actor Zak Prince. Zak finds working with this stunning brunette fun! But someone is out to make mischief from their growing closeness – and soon candid pictures appear in the press...

HIS ONE-NIGHT MISTRESS by Sandra Field

Lia knew that billionaire businessman Seth could destroy her glittering career. But he was so attractive that she succumbed to him – for one night! Eight years on, when he sees Lia in the papers, Seth finds that he has a love-child, and is determined to get her back!

THE ROYAL BABY BARGAIN by Robyn Donald

Prince Caelan Bagaton has found the woman who kidnapped his nephew and now he is going to exact his revenge... For Abby Metcalfe, the only way to continue taking care of the child is to agree to Caelan's demands – and that means marriage!

BACK IN HER HUSBAND'S BED by Melanie Milburne

Seeing Xavier Knightly, the man she divorced five years ago, changes Carli Gresham's life. Their marriage may be dead, but their desire is alive – and three months later Carli tells Xavier a shocking secret! But by wanting her to love him again Xavier faces the biggest battle of his life...

Don't miss out!
On sale 4th November 2005

Available at most branches of WHSmith, Tesco, ASDA, Borders, Eason, Sainsbury's and most bookshops

Visit www.millsandboon.co.uk

breast
cancer
CAMPAIGN

researching the cure

The facts you need to know:

- **One woman in nine** in the United Kingdom will develop breast cancer during her lifetime.

- Each year **40,700** women are newly diagnosed with breast cancer and around **12,800** women will die from the disease. However, survival rates are improving, with on average 77 per cent of women still alive five years later.

- **Men can also suffer from breast cancer**, although currently they make up less than one per cent of all new cases of the disease.

Britain has one of the highest breast cancer death rates in the world. Breast Cancer Campaign wants to understand why and do something about it. Statistics cannot begin to describe the impact that breast cancer has on the lives of those women who are affected by it and on their families and friends.

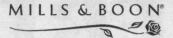

MILLS & BOON®

During the month of October Harlequin Mills & Boon will donate 10p from the sale of every Modern Romance™ series book to help Breast Cancer Campaign in *researching the cure*.

Breast Cancer Campaign's scientific projects look at improving diagnosis and treatment of breast cancer, better understanding how it develops and ultimately either curing the disease or preventing it.

Do your part to help

Visit <u>www.breastcancercampaign.org</u>

And make a donation today.

breast cancer CAMPAIGN

researching the cure

Breast Cancer Campaign is a company limited by guarantee registered in England and Wales. Company No. 05074725. Charity registration No. 299758.
Breast Cancer Campaign, Clifton Centre,110 Clifton Street, London EC2A 4HT.
Tel: 020 7749 3700 Fax: 020 7749 3701 www.breastcancercampaign.org

4 FREE

BOOKS AND A SURPRISE GIFT!

We would like to take this opportunity to thank you for reading this Mills & Boon® book by offering you the chance to take FOUR more specially selected titles from the Modern Romance™ series absolutely FREE! We're also making this offer to introduce you to the benefits of the Reader Service™—

★ FREE home delivery
★ FREE gifts and competitions
★ FREE monthly Newsletter
★ Exclusive Reader Service offers
★ Books available before they're in the shops

Accepting these FREE books and gift places you under no obligation to buy, you may cancel at any time, even after receiving your free shipment. Simply complete your details below and return the entire page to the address below. You don't even need a stamp!

YES! Please send me 4 free Modern Romance books and a surprise gift. I understand that unless you hear from me, I will receive 6 superb new titles every month for just £2.75 each, postage and packing free. I am under no obligation to purchase any books and may cancel my subscription at any time. The free books and gift will be mine to keep in any case.

P5ZED

Ms/Mrs/Miss/Mr ....Initials ....

BLOCK CAPITALS PLEASE

Surname ....

Address ....

....

....Postcode............................

Send this whole page to:
UK: FREEPOST CN81, Croydon, CR9 3WZ

Offer valid in UK only and is not available to current Reader service subscribers to this series. Overseas and Eire please write for details. We reserve the right to refuse an application and applicants must be aged 18 years or over. Only one application per household. Terms and prices subject to change without notice. Offer expires 31st January 2006. As a result of this application, you may receive offers from Harlequin Mills & Boon and other carefully selected companies. If you would prefer not to share in this opportunity please write to The Data Manager, PO Box 676, Richmond, TW9 1WU.

Mills & Boon® is a registered trademark owned by Harlequin Mills & Boon Limited.
Modern Romance™ is being used as a trademark. The Reader Service™ is being used as a trademark.